C000132349

Carys is twenty-four and lives in Shropshire. She's been writing from a young age but this if her first full length novel. One of her big passions in life are films; having studied Film and Creative writing at Wolverhampton University.

When she's not writing, she works for the NHS and loves nothing more than spending time with her family and friends.

NOT ALL STARS SPARKLE

Carys Jones

Not All Stars Sparkle

Vanguard Press

VANGUARD PAPERBACK

© Copyright 2010
CarysJones

The right of CarysJones to be identified as author of
this work has been asserted by her in accordance with the
Copyright, Designs and Patents Act 1988.

All Rights Reserved

No reproduction, copy or transmission of this publication
may be made without written permission.
No paragraph of this publication may be reproduced,
copied or transmitted save with the written permission of the
publisher, or in accordance with the provisions
of the Copyright Act 1956 (as amended).

Any person who commits any unauthorised act in relation to
this publication may be liable to criminal
prosecution and civil claims for damages.

A CIP catalogue record for this title is
available from the British Library.

ISBN 978 184386 655 8

*Vanguard Press is an imprint of
Pegasus Elliot MacKenzie Publishers Ltd.*
www.pegasuspublishers.com

First Published in 2010

**Vanguard Press
Sheraton House Castle Park
Cambridge England**

Printed & Bound in Great Britain

Dedication

To my late Grandmother, Kathleen Morgan, who I know would have been so proud of me.

And to all my family, I can never thank them enough for all the love and support they have given me.

Chapter One

Welcome to Avalon

The dusty road lay empty before him in the fading light. Aiden Connelly rubbed his eyes wearily wondering just how much of his journey was left. Behind him, his little angel, Meegan, slept soundly, oblivious to the dramatic change her life was currently undergoing. His wife stirred in her sleep and Aiden could not help but smile at her tangle of mahogany curls splayed widely around her head. She was usually so immaculate, yet in the throws of sleep she had wrestled around on the uncomfortable seat of the rented car and now resembled a wild woman. This was how Aiden liked his wife, Isla, best. Relaxed, carefree. For so long they had both been so consumed by everything. Even the birth of Meegan had felt like yet another chore, something else to be responsible for, rather than the joy that it should have brought them.

That was why they were here, now. Travelling down an old highway that seemed to be leading them into the middle of nowhere. In reality it was taking them away from it all; the stress, the chaos, the ridiculous pace of the city to a new, quieter life. It was what they needed. Aiden could feel himself becoming a stranger to his family; the hours he needed to spend at the office were increasing daily and he began to question his motives in life and the choices he had made. Initially he got into law for the money, but as he progressed through the course he developed a passion for it. Two years working for one of the most prestigious law firms in Chicago was slowly sucking any positive feeling he had had towards his job out of him. He dealt with high profile cases, they lived in a beautiful penthouse, but Aiden was in serious danger of having no soul.

'The rat race isn't for everyone,' his late father had advised him. 'Happiness is true wealth.' It was rather cliché but Aiden could not help but be inspired by the old man's words. He had grown up in the country, on a farm, and had only happy memories of his childhood. He wanted the same for Meegan. Finding another job was easy considering his previous experience, convincing Isla was the hard part. She loved living in the city, she was always shopping and lunching with friends. As Aiden had pointed out to her, her first love, art, had taken a back seat over the past few years. She had not painted a thing since three summers ago. Admittedly, she had been preoccupied with the arrival of Meegan, but still… Aiden helped her realize that a clean break was what they all needed; surrounded by nature she would undoubtedly be inspired and start painting again in no time.

Dusk was fast turning into night as the headlights of the rented car gleamed upon the approaching roadside.

Avalon - 20 miles

'Not far now,' Aiden said aloud.

'Huh,' Isla stirred, awoken by his voice.

'Not far now, honey. We will soon be in Avalon.'

'Oh good,' she yawned. 'I'm really tired.'

'Tired? You've been asleep for half of the journey!'

'You try sleeping in these seats, it's like lying on a rock!' She snapped her visor down and studied her reflection.

'Ugh, just look at my hair. Thank God it will be dark when we arrive'. Turning to check her daughter, 'Has Meegan been asleep this whole time?'

'Sure has.'

The couple smiled at one another. It felt good. Aiden dared himself to hope that this was all going to be the start of something wonderful.

Less than an hour later the Connelly family pulled into the driveway of their new home. After driving down what Aiden had assumed was the high street, he had quickly located his new neighborhood. Avalon was a small, sparse town; he had only spotted one convenience store, along with two churches, a hair salon, a doctor's surgery and a florist. From various flyers dotted around he had quickly assessed that there was a high school nearby with an impending football match that was obviously of great importance to the community. Given that they didn't seem to have much else going on, this did not surprise him. He had yet to locate his new offices, Cope and May Attorneys at Law, but he had a few days yet before he had to start work so that could wait. Given the size of Avalon he doubted that they would be far away.

'Well...it's quaint,' Isla stood surveying the wooden one-storey property before her. It had certainly seen better days. Like an ageing movie star, if you looked hard enough you could still see the glimmer of something special; that many years ago it was something magnificent but now the years had performed their devastating trick and what was once glorious was now faded and lackluster. Isla imagined that the house had once been a beautiful blue, as bright and wonderful as a summer's day, but that blue had dulled to a sad shade of grey. The white of the windows had yellowed and the front lawn exposed more dirt than grass. It really was a far cry from the modern, immaculate penthouse she had left behind. It was all she could do not to burst into tears. She hoped that tomorrow things might seem brighter but she knew that in the harsh light of day even more flaws would be exposed to her. This was Aiden's dream, not hers. But she loved him, and she loved Meegan. In her heart she knew that this had to work; it was their last chance.

'It certainly has character,' Aiden wrapped a strong arm around his wife's delicate shoulders. Instinctively she leant into him.

'You can paint the house, decorate it inside. Do whatever you like. Just think how great it will feel to be doing something creative again.'

'And the garden?'

13

'Well now I'm working less I'll do the garden up a real treat. Get a jungle gym for Meegan, maybe a small pond for you, you've always been saying how you would love to have some fish, that you find water soothing.'

Isla smiled, and it was genuine. She could feel the clean air of Avalon filling up her lungs and it felt good. Above her the night sky sparkled and she was amazed at how many stars she could see.

'I think we can make this work,' she told her husband hopefully.

'I know we can, hun. You, me and Meegan, it will be wonderful.'

'Dada,' Meegan called from the car, the cool breeze from the open car doors awakening her from her slumber.

'Hey, princess,' Aiden cooed as he lifted her from her car seat. 'Do you like your new home?' He turned the tiny toddler to face the house and she rubbed her hazel eyes sleepily.

'Night, night,' she murmured grumpily, indicating that she wanted to sleep.

'I second that,' Isla yawned.

'Hopefully the movers put everything in the right place.'

Aiden lay in bed counting the cracks on the ceiling. Isla was already fast asleep. The gentle hum of crickets gave a comforting soundtrack to his muddle of thoughts. The house needed a lot of work; the realtor had been very clear about that and he wasn't lying. The profit they had made on the penthouse would more than cover any costs for maintenance work. Before she had slipped into that oh so wonderful world of dreams, Isla had asked him why he had chosen to move to Avalon of all the towns in America. She had drifted to sleep before he could respond, and lying awake next to her, a good hour later, he was still struggling to find an answer.

After three days of intense unpacking, Aiden pulled up outside Cope and May Attorneys at Law. It hadn't taken him long to locate the modest office since Avalon was so small and it was the only local law firm. Two days previous he had enquired about his future workplace whilst buying groceries and the clerk had been more than helpful, informing him how the business was once run by Edmond Cope and Howard May, but since Howard's death three years ago Edmond had been going it alone. Apparently he managed fine at first, but even a town as small as Avalon has its fair share of legal affairs that need tending to so, apparently reluctantly, he advertised for a new partner. This revelation made Aiden a little anxious; Mr. Cope probably had his own way of doing things and would no doubt take all the better cases for himself. If there were any cases at all. Even though he had been there for just a few days, Aiden was already noticing that the pace of life in Avalon was remarkably slow; it was the kind of place where you didn't bother locking your doors and would happily let your kids play out on the front lawn.

Cope and May was located between Smith's Pharmacy and Redd Books. In total his journey to work had taken him about ten minutes. Aiden liked the thought of being able to go home for dinner, in Chicago his commute had taken two hours in total. At night he was almost always too exhausted to do anything besides collapse on his bed. Most nights he came home way past Meegan's bedtime, much to Isla's annoyance. The past three nights, being there to bath his little girl and read her a goodnight story, had been amazing. He had no idea how much he had been missing out on and sacrificing for his job. Even though he knew that working in Avalon would be worlds away from what he was used to he knew that he was already reaping the benefits. Taking a deep breath he braced himself and walked through the glass front door to the cheerful chimes of a small bell.

'Good morning,' a cheerful elderly lady seated at a mahogany desk along the far wall greeted him. Her ashen hair sat atop her wrinkled face like a giant choux bun. Her small frame was adorned with a tight, crisp, white shirt and her glasses hung down from a chain around her neck. The words 'prim and proper' sprang to Aiden's mind.

'Well good morning, I'm Aiden Connelly.'

'Ah, Mr. Connelly. How lovely to meet you! I'm Betty Hales, I've been secretary here for the past twenty years. Oh, it is most exciting to have you here working with us. Please, do take a seat, I'll let Edmond, Mr. Cope, know that you are here.'

Aiden obliged and settled himself on one of the two battered leather couches that occupied the waiting room. There was a coffee table littered with magazines, ranging from Gardening Monthly to Vogue, all clearly out of date. The hardwood flooring was surprisingly tasteful and the walls were painted a calming pale shade of green. Aiden guessed that the room had recently been decorated, albeit the ancient seeming furniture, including the leather couches, one of which he was rapidly sinking into. He hoisted himself up using the arm into a less comfortable looking position.

'Oh, Mr. Copes,' Betty had pressed the intercom on her desk. 'I have Mr. Connelly for you.'

'Send him in.'

'In you go then, dear. Best of luck,' she smiled. Aiden nodded and lifted himself up from the absorbing couch and entered the door beside Betty's desk, which he assumed was the office as the only other door in the room was marked 'lavatory'.

The main office was a large room, painted in the same soothing green as the waiting area. Two large desks with computers occupied a majority of the space and numerous filing cabinets lined two of the walls. The desk nearest to the door was immaculate whilst the other was awash with papers and files. A man hastily got up from the cluttered desk and quickly smoothed down his blue shirt.

Edmond Copes was getting on in years. As his hairline decreased his waistline expanded until now he was basically bald and quite rotund. It was common knowledge that he enjoyed his drink; if Aiden played his cards right he would learn of the generous amount of liquor the old man kept in his desk drawer. It had been common practice for himself and his old partner, Howard May, to indulge in an afternoon tipple when work was slow. Since Howard's death, the afternoon tipple had increased to occasionally include mornings too. Three years was a long time to be in an office alone and Edmond was a sociable man. He loved nothing more than entertaining his large family at his equally large home. In all honesty he had opened up the position for a new partner out of loneliness rather than necessity. When he read Aiden's profile he could scarcely believe his luck; a young hotshot lawyer wanting to work in Avalon? With his pending retirement looming he was hoping that Aiden may well indeed be someone whom could take over the business. But this was all jumping the gun somewhat. Edmond stuck out his podgy hand and Aiden shook it enthusiastically.

'Edmond Copes, welcome, welcome!'

'Thank you, Mr. Copes.'

'Please, Edmond, Mr. Copes was my father! Your desk is there, my boy, do take time to familiarise yourself with it. The computer is all set up, she may not look it but Betty is a whiz with technology!'

Aiden smiled but was inwardly flinching at the 'my boy' comment.

'I would give you a tour of the place but there isn't much to see. There is the waiting area where Betty is, the restrooms and here, the Epi-centre of it all! I expect you are used to much bigger places but this serves us all right.'

'Bigger is not always better.'

'True, true.'

'So…' Edmond was still standing in the centre of the room, his ample chest puffed out in grandeur. 'Cope and May has been serving the legal needs of Avalon for a good thirty years come this fall. I myself founding the company, along with my dear friend and colleague Howard May, God rest his soul. We went to college together you see, studied law, wanted to make a change and that. We thought about going to work in the city but were perhaps too attached to our families and what not to leave. But the town has been good to us; we are never short of work.'

'Glad to hear it.'

'That was why the position of partner came up. I was getting bogged down by it all; some days I wasn't getting home until 6pm! The wife said enough is enough! I work to live, I don't live to work. You know, son?'

'I hear you loud and clear.'

'Good, good,' Edmond now settled himself once more at his desk.

'When I read your profile I knew you could handle things here; will most likely seem a doddle compared to what you had to deal with in the city. The thing is to remember that Avalon is full of good people, for the most part. There is the odd bad apple but most cases are property disputes, drunken brawls, that kind of thing. Nothing too wayward. It may seem menial at times but it is ultimately rewarding. Like I said, it is a town full of good people and they are always more than grateful for our help. Only the other day Mrs. McKenzie from the small farm down the road sent me a basket of lovely apples to thank me for helping her husband when he got sentenced a DUI.'

Aiden nodded.

'We get a lot of DUIs. Folk just don't think, but we have a good relationship with the local law enforcement who keeps us up to speed on things. Buck Fern is the local Sheriff and has been as long as I can remember. Straight as an arrow that man. Folks round here respect him and that's important in keeping the peace and all that. I'll get him to pop by later this week; no doubt he'll be keen to meet you.'

'Yes, of course.'

'You got family, Mr. Connelly?'

'Yes, a wife and daughter.' Aiden's reply clearly pleased Edmond. 'And please, call me Aiden,' he added.

'Well, Aiden, how old is your little ray of sunshine?'

'Meegan turns two next month.'

'Two, how wonderful! My grandson Grant was two just last week. Lovely age. Well, I suppose I need to stop smacking my gums with you and get down to working. We are starting to sound like a couple of hens with our cackling!'

Aiden could feel himself warming towards the old man. You couldn't help but like him.

'But first things first, you cannot work without coffee,' Edmond pressed the intercom on his desk.

'Betty, my dear'.

'Yes, Mr. Cope,' her response came back crackly through the machine.

'Can we have two coffees,' to Aiden, whispered, 'you do drink coffee, son?' Aiden nodded. 'Yes, two coffees please, Betty.'

'Right away.'
'Thank you, my dear.'

After Betty has bustled in with two steaming coffees and a plate of biscuits, Edmond handed Aiden a thin brown file. On the front it read;

White, Brandy
Case no. 2315

Aiden assumed it was a routine DUI and was about to read the notes when Edmond stopped him.

'Now that there is an unusual case. It is pretty much open, shut, not much to be done. I'm giving it to you as I thought you would have experience in that sort of thing, and being new to town, folk might not want you delving into their personal matters quite so fast.'

Intrigued, Aiden opened the file.

'A murder case?' he could not conceal his shock. A shiver of excitement ran down his spine. He was prepared to deal with domestic disputes, unruly neighbors, but a murder! This was legal gold!

'Don't get too excited there, Aiden. Like I said, open, shut. Mrs. White is a resident here in Avalon; we represent her as an obligation not through choice. She has already confessed to the crime and is awaiting sentencing over at Eastham Ladies Penitentiary, about twenty miles east of here.'

'I see,' Aiden muttered, his eyes scanning over the records before him.

'She murdered her husband in cold blood, terrible matter. ShoOK the town to its core. He was a beloved town hero. She must have been possessed by the devil himself to do such a thing.'

'When is the hearing?'

'Three weeks from now. You just need to go over, give her legal support, explain what will likely occur after her guilty plea.'

'So, she is down for first degree murder?'

'Yes, sir.'

'So under state law...?'

'It will be the death penalty, son. No messing about here.'

'My God, she's only twenty-four.'

'It ain't pretty, son. Murder never is. If you feel this case is a little too heavy for you, just say. Personally, I knew Brandon and know his father well, we go to the same church. It wouldn't feel right representing Mrs. White myself. I'm sure you understand.'

'Yeah.'

'That is the downside of working in such a small town. You know pretty much everyone who walks through them doors and it is hard not to be attached or emotionally involved. Especially this case. Everyone round here is still reeling from it all.'

'Any idea why she did it?'

'None at all. As her lawyer I guess it is your job to sniff that out. That's if you want the case?'

'Yeah, yes, of course! I dealt with a lot of murder suspects in Chicago so it is not a problem at all.'

'Well then, I most heartily welcome you to Cope and May Attorneys at Law. May we enjoy a long and prosperous working relationship together.' Edmond raised his coffee mug in celebration, as did Aiden. In his mind, Edmond was all too aware of the bottle of sweet, sweet liquor nestling just inches from him but reasoned it was too early on in his relationship with Aiden to break it out, even when a toast was in order. Besides, it was only half past nine in the morning. To drink before noon was something only winos did.

Aiden spent the rest of the day researching the Brandy White case. Edmond had been right when he had said that it was open, shut. Mrs. White had confessed to the murder of her husband almost immediately; in fact she had been the one who had dialed 911. He had seen this kind of thing before, a domestic argument gotten out of hand. They had only intended to fire a warning shot. The police report made for chilling reading; Mr. White had been stabbed in the chest six times. Mrs. White was apparently covered in his blood and hysterical when police arrived at the scene. Aiden made a call to Eastham to arrange a visit for the following day.

It was early afternoon and Aiden felt that he was all wrapped up with his work and prepared for his visit to Brandy the next day. Edmond must have sensed this as at 2pm he looked over from his desk; he had furiously been typing at his computer pretty much all day, apart from the occasional call to Betty for coffee.

'Fancy calling it a day, Aiden? I've got Mr. and Mrs. Johnson in here this afternoon to discuss setting up a will so I'll be needing the office to myself anyways.'

'Only if you are sure?'

'Yes, it's fine. There are no strict hours here, just get the work done. So you are popping over to Eastham tomorrow?'

'Sure am.'

'I like your style, just dive right in. If you could pop by on your way back, just to report in and that?'

'Of course.'

'Wonderful, Betty has some directions to Eastham in her desk; I'm sure she won't mind fishing those out for you.'

Aiden said his goodbyes, gathered up his briefcase and jacket and went out to talk to Betty. Left alone, Edmond felt that he more than deserved the small drink which he was already pouring for himself.

'Terrible business,' Betty was shaking her head as she riffled through her drawer looking for the directions.

'He was a lovely young man, so handsome. And she…well, beauty clearly is more than skin deep. Ah, here it is,' she handed Aiden a crumpled piece of typed paper with a faded map on the back.

'I'm sorry it isn't very clear, dear. We rarely have the need to visit the ladies' prison you see. Usually the men making all the trouble, no offence.'

'None taken.'

'If you get stranded just give me a call. I've lived here all my life and know my way around Avalon like the back of my hand.'

'Thanks, I will.'

'Well, best of luck with your first case, Mr. Connelly. Not that you'll need it.'

'Thank you, Betty.'

Aiden was satisfied with his first day at work. He had a decent case, he was leaving at a very reasonable hour. He couldn't wait to get home and spend the evening with his wife and daughter.

'Well, I could certainly get used to this!' Isla exclaimed as her husband entered the kitchen at 2:30pm.

'On work days I'm not used to seeing you during daylight hours!'

'I know, great isn't it?' Aiden beamed as he kissed his wife on the cheek.

'And how is Daddy's favorite girl?' Meegan was sat in her high chair and squealed with excitement when she saw Aiden.

'She's been helping Mommy wash up.'

'Good girl,' he ruffled her fine hair and placed his briefcase down on the table.

'So, good day?'

'Yeah, really good. The place is small but I expected that. I really like the guy, Edmond Copes, seems really genuine.'

'You should invite him round for dinner. I take it he is married?'

'Whoa, get you, Suzie Homemaker! Since when do we invite people round for dinner? Four days in Avalon and you are a changed woman!'

'Gimme a break,' Isla dried her hands on the tea towel and playfully flicked him with it.

'We are in a new town. It will be good for us to make friends with people. Besides, with you working I'm going to get lonely and be in need of adult companionship. There is only so much baby talk I can handle.'

'Well I'll ask him then, although I don't want to blur the lines between work and home.'

'This isn't Chicago, Aid. People here aren't ruthless and spineless, they are kind.'

'What makes you so sure?'

'Well, since being here I've been to the grocery store and today the salon and everyone is always super nice, although they keep inviting me to church…'

'See'

'What?'

'They are already trying to ram their belief system down our throats.'

'Don't be so silly. They are just trying to make us feel part of the community. We are going on Sunday. End of.'

'What?' Aiden made a mock face of disgust at Meegan who burst into fits of giggles.

'It will be good for us. Besides, Meegan has never even been christened.'

'Since when were you interested in all that religious stuff?'

'Jeeze, Aid, I'm just trying to make a good impression. While you are at work I've got to be here holding down the fort and I don't want us to be the heathen family who don't attend church. If we plan on settling here we are going to need friends.' Isla's hands were now placed firmly on her hips as she stared him down.

'I'm just joshing you, honey. Of course I'll go church Sunday. I need to start making contacts of my own. Edmond was saying how he'd introduce me to the local sheriff soon.'

'Sounds good. So was it all cattle ownership suits and someone erecting a fence on another's lawn?'

'Actually, I got a murder case.' Isla's eyes widened.

'What, here? I thought this was a safe place!'

'It is, it is. I haven't established much yet, but it seems a simple domestic case. Wife stabs husband in a frenzy'.

'I can relate to that,' Isla teased.

'It is nothing I haven't dealt with before. I'm going to meet the suspect tomorrow.'

'Where?'

'Local women's prison. I'll let you know what it's like, for when they take you in for losing it with me.'

'The nerve!' Isla threw the tea towel from beside her at Aiden but he caught it mid-air.

'Nice try,' he laughed. Meegan joined in the laughing.

'Well, I am busy tomorrow, too.'

'Oh yeah?'

'Meegan and I are going to get beautified at the local salon. They were more than happy for me to take her there whilst I got my hair done. Could never have done that in Chicago.'

'See, we are already reaping the benefits. I'm home, you are now a God-fearing housewife…'

'And since you are home, you can prepare dinner tonight with me for a change.'

'What is on the menu for chez Connelly?'

'Spaghetti Bolognese.'

'Ah, bellisimo'!

That evening was one of the most pleasant Aiden had experienced in a long time. He cooked dinner with his wife, played with his daughter and as the sun set he didn't feel exhausted and drained, he felt alive. He sprawled himself across the couch, glass of wine in hand, surrounded by cardboard boxes in various stages of unpacking. The house was slowly starting to come together and feel like home. Isla had already started to paint some of the walls which made a huge difference. A little time and a little love and it would be amazing. He looked out into the garden wistfully, imagining summer barbeques with friends, Meegan playing happily with Edmond's grandson, Grant. The men enjoying some ice cold beers, the women gossiping over some wine. Isla seemed to be settling in which was good news. This was all such a culture shock for her but she was taking it really well. Aiden assumed that finding the beauty salon had made a big impact on her mood. His wife loved to get pampered and shop. Since shopping was confined to the few stores Avalon had to offer she would have to make do with pampering for now, not that he was complaining.

'You coming to bed, baby?' Isla asked from the doorway.

Aiden craned his neck to see her and noticed a familiar, knowing glint in her eyes. He sprang up from the couch and bounded upstairs like an excited schoolboy. Oh yes, he most certainly could get used to this.

Chapter Two

First Encounters

From the little research that Aiden had done, he knew that Eastham Ladies Penitentiary was a maximum security prison for the most serious of offenders. This didn't unnerve him too much as he had expected as much. In his ignorance he felt mildly relieved that it was a female prison, knowing how much more intimidated he would feel about his impending visit if it were a male prison. He had seen one too many prison movies and avoided male prisons as much as he could.

The previous night he had enjoyed a deep, dreamless sleep and had awoken so refreshed that he truly felt that he could take on the world. Full of optimism he kissed his wife and daughter goodbye and with Betty's directions, headed out to Eastham.

The prison was not hard to find, it was well signposted for pretty much the entire journey. Aiden had been driving along empty roads that seemed to lead to nowhere for a good forty minutes when a huge, grey castle appeared on the horizon. Instead of a moat there were rolling fields with various layers of electrical fencing. The gate consisted of dozens of barriers and enforced metal doors which grudgingly slid open when he stated his name and purpose to the hard-faced security man. From a distance Eastham seemed strangely beautiful. A huge blot on the endless expanse of rolling prairies, it looked like something from another world. Aiden half-expected to be greeted by Spock as he parked up and headed towards yet another guarded entrance.

All the outer walls were a dense grey, the only fleck of colour coming from the blue uniform worn by the guards.

Despite being surrounded by luscious acres of green grass none grew within the walls of the immense prison. Aiden wondered if this was a result of all the electrical fencing, or if nature just knew that she was not welcome here. This was a place for those who did not deserve to hear the sweet lullaby of birdsong, or breathe in the luscious scent of a blooming flower. Here, the condemned were at the last outpost before hell, but no doubt many felt like they were already there. Whilst from a distance Eastham looked impressive, once inside you realized just how imposing a structure can really be. Aiden had only just arrived but was already looking forward to being able to drive away.

'Freedom', he mused to himself, 'is much too underrated'.

Inside was not much better. The air felt decidedly cooler and the indifferent grey of the stone had crept along the interior walls in the form of paint. Green doors, though the colour of baby sick, were a welcome break from the dismal decorating. Aiden was led along countless corridors, his footsteps echoing on the plastic tiled floors. He was ushered through so many security gates that he began to worry if he was ever going to be able to get back out.

'Prisoner 929 is in maximum security.' The burly female guard had told him when he had finally made it to reception, her voice monotonous as if she had forgotten how to express emotion. He was currently being led by another, equally ample female form, down a labyrinth of corridors. His palms were sweaty and his attempts to make small talk had not even been acknowledged. The women who worked there were tough; he supposed that they had to be. But no matter how tough they were, he knew that they would be no match for what lay behind the locked doors which they were now passing by. Aiden had expected hands grasping through railings, voices crying out their innocence, but all was quiet. Those cells he passed where you could see in, the lone occupants were sat, sometimes reading, sometimes just staring into space; none so much as fluttered an eyelid as he clomped past.

Finally he was motioned into a small room where one wall was made entirely of Perspex glass. Beyond the glass, there was a lone chair facing him which was flanked by two guards. On Aiden's side of the glass there was a basic desk and a plastic chair.

'929 will be with you shortly', the woman told him. 'I'll wait for you outside.'

Aiden nodded and thanked her but she was already gone before the words had even left his mouth. He moved the chair and positioned himself opposite the other currently vacant chair. Placing his briefcase on the desk he took out a Dictaphone and a notebook. He had no idea what to expect from Prisoner 929.

'Are you ready?' one of the guards asked from the other side. Aiden merely nodded in response.

'Send her in!' the other guard yelled. Her. It was the first acknowledgment that Brandy White was indeed a woman and not just a number.

Prisoner 929 was ushered into the room. She was wearing a garish orange jumpsuit and her hands were handcuffed. Eyes trained to the floor she obediently followed the guard's instructions and sat herself down in the chair opposite Aiden. Still she did not look up. She placed her cuffed hands in her lap and he noticed how tiny they were. The thick metal bracelets overwhelmed her small wrists so much so that he wondered if she could easily free herself from her constraints if she so desired. Not that the guards needed to worry if she did get free. When she shuffled in Aiden assessed that she was no more than five foot one and incredibly petite in build. They could easily lift her up with one arm. Her bleached blonde hair fell in waves upon her shoulders and down her back. She appeared like a fairy child, not a murdering monster. Finally she raised her eyes to meet his and Aiden looked upon his first client in Avalon.

His breath caught in his throat for a moment as he gazed at Brandy White. She was devastatingly beautiful. Her lips were a deep red, plump and permanently pouting, the skin which was exposed on her face and hands was as white and as delicate as the finest china. Her face was a perfect heart shape, with a delicate button nose. But it was her eyes which had captivated Aiden. They were so round and wide in her little head, the colour of autumn leaves, fringed with dark, curled lashes. Her eyes bore into his, questioning, confused.

'Mrs. White, I am your attorney, my name is Aiden Connelly.' He noticed her relax at his introduction.

'How do you do, Mr. Connelly?' her voice was soft and melodic, laced in a lazy southern drawl. 'I thought you might be a priest.'

'A priest?'

'Yes, sir. I asked them if I could see a priest but I haven't been visited yet.'

'Why do you want to see a priest?'

Brandy seemed alarmed by his question.

'Why, Mr. Connelly, I have not been to church in well over a month, it is a matter of urgency that I see a priest, my immortal soul is at stake!' He wondered if she was joking but he could tell by her anxiety that she was being quite earnest.

'Well then, I will see if I can set that up for you, Mrs. White.'

'Please, call me Brandy. It just doesn't feel right being called Mrs. White.'

'Very well, Brandy, I am here to represent your case at your upcoming trial. I will need to go over details of the event with you, verify your statement with the one you gave to the police. If you have any questions at all...'

'Are you from Avalon?' she interrupted.

'Yes, I am.' She furrowed her brow.

'I do not mean to be rude, Mr. Connelly, but I don't recall ever seeing you around and Avalon is a mighty small place.'

'I'm new, moved there less than a week ago.' He felt uncomfortable that the conversation was moving towards him; it was important to never reveal personal information to clients.

'Must be different from living in a big city.'

'City?' he nervously wondered how she could possibly know where he was from.

'Relax,' she smiled, noticing his tense expression. 'Your suit gave you away. You can't buy smart suits like that in Avalon, and if you did you would find little occasion to wear them. In all honesty I'm mighty touched that you made such an effort to come and see little old me!'

He searched for the cynicism in her comment, but saw only a warm smile and kind, yet frightened eyes.

'Well, let us get down to it,' Aiden leant and retrieved a file from his briefcase and switched on the Dictaphone.

'Can you please just state your name and age, for the recording?'

'Brandy White. I'm twenty four.'

'Thank you. So on April 6th of this year, you were charged with the murder of your husband, Brandon White.'

'Yes, sir.'

'Records state that you yourself made the distress call to 911 at approximately 11:23pm.' Brandy nodded.

'Can you please answer vocally for the recording?'

'Oh, yes, I made the call.'

'Did you call because you regretted what had just happened?'

'Oh no, sir. I waited until he was dead, then called.'

'So, you admit that you deliberately stabbed your husband,' he checked his notes, 'six times in the back and chest?'

'Yes.'

'Waiting until he was dead and then calling 911?'

'Yes.'

'Would you say that you were of sound mind when the incident occurred?'

'Oh yes, for the first time in my life I saw things clearly.' Aiden found her responses puzzling and was beginning to question the young woman's sanity. She did not appear to be the least bit remorseful and was quick to admit her guilt. On all accounts she should come across as callous and cold, but there was a warmth in her eyes and in her smile that suggested that meditated murder was something she could never had committed, even in her wildest dreams.

'Was the murder premeditated?'

Brandy flushed with embarrassment and Aiden realized that she had not fully understood his question. 'Was it planned out?'

'Yes and no.'

29

'Can you be clearer, please?'

'Well, I knew it had to be done, I just didn't know when until the opportunity arose. So I guess that it was sort of planned.'

'OK', Aiden jotted down a few notes. 'So that you understand, Brandy, you have pleaded guilty to the murder of Brandon White and say that you did this of your own free will whilst of sound mind.'

'Uh huh.'

'This means that at your trial, if the judge is satisfied that you are guilty of first degree murder, under state law, you will receive the death penalty.' Aiden felt sick to his stomach as he said it. Brandy nodded in understanding and tears pricked her eyes but did not wash down upon her cheeks. She took a deep breath, quickly composing herself.

'I am happy to accept the consequences for my actions.' There was something bizarrely noble about her attitude.

'Very well, then. As your attorney you can address any questions you have to me.'

'Oh good, since no one talks to me in here. I've been getting kind of lonely,' a sadness seemed to envelope her tiny frame. Aiden wondered if the reality of what she had done was beginning to set in.

'Well, I'll come back in a few days so that we can discuss things further.'

'I'd like that,' she smiled. The guards moved forward as their time together came to an end, ready to escort Prisoner 929 back to her cell.

'Will you be attending church this Sunday, Mr. Connelly?' Her question caught him off guard.

'Why yes, I believe I will be.'

'Well then be sure to send Father West my regards.' With that she left the room and the atmosphere suddenly grew much more oppressive. She was a light and Aiden felt a pang of guilt that he would be assisting in helping to extinguish it.

As Aiden passed through the security gates and started his journey back to Avalon he reflected upon his first meeting with Brandy. During his career in law he had encountered many men and women accused of murder, some guilty, some not so guilty. They varied in age, ethnic background, financial status, but one trait that they all had in common was that when you were with them, no matter what they were saying, be it professing their innocence or describing the murder in gruesome detail, there was always an element of anger, and dare Aiden say, evil, lurking behind their eyes. Whilst these people may seem perfectly normal on the outside, he could always sense that malignant rage and malice which would drive them to do something as terrible as taking another life. What puzzled him about Brandy was that in her eyes all he saw was sadness. Something about the case just wasn't adding up.

Besides the fact that she did not seem in any way monstrous, which was a silly conclusion anyway, she was more than likely putting on a show for Aiden, hiding her true self. But even if that were the case, there were the simple physics of it all. Brandy White was tiny; she could not weigh more than 112 pounds. How had she managed to overpower her husband? Perhaps he was enfeebled? Had caring for a sick husband driven her to madness? It was possible. Aiden noted that he needed to do more background research on Brandon White. He needed to know why a seemingly sweet and innocent woman would murder her own husband in cold blood and then so freely admit to it.

His mind had been racing so much that Aiden had failed to realize that he was already back in Avalon. The sky had now clouded over with the threat of rain. A small voice in the back of his mind reminded him that this was tornado country but he dismissed it. He parked up outside Cope and May; he was quickly getting to know his way around town.

'Well, hello, Mr. Connelly,' Betty greeted him warmly as his arrival was declared through the gentle jingle at the door.
'Hello, Betty, how are you today?'
'Very well, thank you, dear. And yourself? Did you find Eastham alright?'

'Oh yes, no trouble at all,' he was about to walk into the office when he added, 'your directions really helped.' Betty beamed at this, and, maybe he imagined it, seemed to blush slightly. Isla was always teasing Aiden about his effect on women but he failed to notice it. Looking back, he reasoned that he had never chatted a woman up before, had never needed to as they seemed more than happy to approach him. Isla had cornered him at a mutual friend's party when they were at college together. She later told him that she only did it because he looked like James Dean. Not that Aiden was complaining. Yes, he had never been short of female attention and had never pursued a woman. The macho side of him would have welcomed the challenge of the chase, but the lazier side felt why run after what you already have, on a plate no less?

'Hey there, champ!' Edmond was at his desk typing away, surrounded by stacks of paper and three empty coffee mugs. He was clearly having a busy day.

'How did it go at Eastham?'

'It went well,' Aiden said as he sat down and switched on his computer, ready to write up his report of his first meeting with Brandy.

'Although...' he stopped himself from going further. Edmond would surely think him a fool if he confessed to his mixed feelings about the case.

'Although?'

'No, nothing,' Aiden waved his hand dismissively.

'No, go on, son. You can talk freely here, you are amongst friends.'

Aiden took a deep breath.

'Brandy White, she is so, you know, small? And very well spoken. She even expressed her desire to see a priest. She just doesn't fit the stereotypical role of a cold killer.'

Edmond stiffened in his chair and locked eyes with Aiden. His face was set in a stern expression.

'Brandon White was a good, decent man. A pillar of the community. Small she may be but her wickedness knows no bounds. I've no doubt she fluttered her eyelashes and pouted her big red lips. To look at, you would think she was the sweetest thing. Do not be taken in by her. She is beautiful, but deadly. Keep your distance.'

Aiden was surprised by Edmond's hostile tone and knew better than to push the conversation further.

'You are right, of course,' Edmond relaxed at this and his eyes drifted back to his computer screen. 'I just need to do some more research on the case; I need to get more background on Mr. White.'

'Well, you won't be short of information around here. He's a local hero, led his high school football team, the Avalon Angels, to win their first ever State Championship. It was wonderful. He attended church every Sunday without fail and worked for his father, Clyde, over at his timber company. He was Clyde's only son, he has been in pieces ever since.'

Aiden just nodded as he jotted down football, church and timber. He wanted to get a better idea of who Brandon was. Everyone in Avalon seemed to idolize him, but if he was such a great man, why would his young, beautiful wife kill him? If a story like this had occurred in Chicago the papers would have had a field day.

'Was there a lot of media coverage on the murder?'

'Oh, tonnes. The local paper, of course, and once word got out about what had happened more and more started turning up and asking questions. Things have died down a bit lately but I expect the media circus will come to town again around the trial. You best be ready, my boy. Once they get wind that you are her lawyer they will come sniffing round and asking questions. It is always best just to keep schtum'.

'Yes, don't worry, I won't say anything to the press,' he added newspapers to his list.

'Good lad.'

'Before I forget, my wife, Isla, would like to have yourself and your wife round for dinner one night.'

'Oh how splendid!' Edmond smiled ear to ear. 'I'll have a word with Mrs. Copes tonight. Although I should warn you, she does like a drink or two.'

The clouds still hung heavy with the threat of rain when Aiden pulled into his driveway. He had spent the afternoon going over his notes and listening to the audio recording of his meeting with Brandy. He had assembled a number of questions for when he next went to visit the prison and was determined to find out more about her deceased husband, Brandon.

The sweet smell of apple pie floated on the air and enticed his senses. He hoped that the delicious aroma was coming from his own home but did not want to get his hopes up as it would be completely out of character for Isla to bake.

To Aiden's delight, when he entered the kitchen he was greeted by a glorious pie sitting proudly in the centre of the table.

'Well, well,' he called out. Meegan came hurrying in to greet him, throwing herself clumsily into his legs for a hug.

'Hey, tiny dancer,' he scooped her up in his arms and noted how quickly she was growing and gaining weight these days. He was thankful to now be having the chance to savour each and every precious moment of all her too fleeting childhood.

'Pie, pie!' she squealed, pointing over at the table.

'Yes, I can see a lovely pie. Did Mommy make it?'

'And me!'

'Oh, of course, and you.'

'She helped crush apples,' Isla informed him as she entered the kitchen.

'Clever girl,' Meegan was beaming with pride.

'How was work?'

Aiden set his daughter down and she ran off into the living room. He admired the pie again and gave his wife an approving smile.

'Well this is certainly nice to come home to. Makes a change from take-out!'

'The nearest take-out is two towns over so you better get used to good old home cooking!'

'Work was good thanks, hun. Went to the prison, it was quite interesting. I can't make her out.'

'Who?'

'The suspect. She seems, well, not like a killer.'

'But she is though, isn't she?'

'Well, yes, she confessed.'

'There you go then. Don't go over-thinking it. Just enjoy handling a simple case,' Isla began to lay the table for dinner.

'So what delicacy have you whipped up for tonight?'

'Macaroni and cheese.'

'Oh,' Aiden found it hard to conceal his disappointment at the meal which had been his staple diet whilst a struggling student.

'I know, it isn't the most exciting but the pie took forever, I'm still getting used to this whole Stepford Wives scenario.'

'I'm grateful, don't get me wrong. I love mac and cheese, and I know Meegan is crazy for it. Thanks,' he went over and planted a kiss on her cheek.

'So, what do you think?' Isla stepped back from him and held her hands out expectantly, her face was full of excitement.

'So?' Aiden was confused.

'Come on Aid, don't kid, you like it right?'

'Erm…' he looked his wife up and down, unsure what the answer she was looking for was.

'God, Aid!' her tone made it clear he had given a very wrong answer.

'My hair, jeeze! I had my hair done, remember? Shorter, new colour. God, you just live in your own little world, just like you did in Chicago!' her face was flush with anger, and now that she mentioned it, her hair did look a bit different.

'Hey,' Aiden was getting defensive, 'there is no need to be like that. I've just got in; give me chance to get myself together.'

'There was a time when you would notice something like that straight away!'

'Well, excuse me for not being the most perceptive man in the world! Your hair looks great, Isla. Sorry I didn't notice it the second you walked into the room. Maybe you shouldn't have distracted me with the pie if you wanted to be the centre of attention!'

'Oh, that's right, I think it's all about me,' her hands were folded across her chest, her eyes locked onto Aiden in a death stare and her voice was now eerily calm. He hated women's mood swings. He hated arguing because he knew that whatever he said was inevitably going to be the wrong answer.

'It usually is always about you.'

35

Now her eyes bulged with rage and the calmness was once again swept away by her anger.

'Oh yes, Aid. Me, me me! We are here because of ME! Isn't that right? How dare you! I moved *my life* for *you*. And this is how you repay me? Great! I'm trying my best to keep it together, this place is so unbelievably backwards, getting my hair done at least helps me get some sense of normality.'

'Do you know how shallow that sounds?'

'I don't care! I'm here and I'm really trying. I don't want to become some housewife who fades into the background of your life!'

'Isla, I see you. All I could think when I came in was how proud I was of you baking a pie, which is so much more important to me than your hair being immaculate. That is why we are here, to get our values right. You look beautiful to me no matter what. I don't want Meegan to grow up being image-obsessed. I don't want her to get sick like you did.'

Isla's eyes grew teary at the mention of her battle with anorexia, which while a distant memory, still had the power to cut her like a knife. Aiden crossed the space between them which was littered with insults and spite. He held his wife in his arms and kissed her new hair.

'You look beautiful, baby, you always do.' She was now crying into his shoulder.

'Mommy?' Meegan was looking up at them, bewilderment streaked across her little face and tears streaking her podgy cheeks.

'Oh, baby girl,' Isla gasped, hurriedly wiping the tears from her own cheeks.

'What…is…wrong?' the little girl sobbed, the confusion of seeing her mother cry overwhelming her.

'Nothing, honey,' Isla was now hugging her little girl as her sobs turned into hiccups.

'Daddy told Mommy he was going to eat the whole pie because it looks so good and I'm very hungry,' Aiden offered as an explanation.

'No!' Meegan screamed and started hitting his legs in fury.

'Hey,' he protested, grabbing her little arms mid-punch. 'I'm sure that there is enough for us all to share, you and Mommy did a great job and I'm very proud.'

Isla smiled warmly at them both.

'And doesn't Mommy look super pretty with her hair?'

'Oh yes,' Meegan was now smiling again. Aiden felt exhausted, living with two women was far from easy.

'They make my nails pink!' she showed her dad her tiny nails which now glistened and sparkled. He hid his true feelings with a smile as he couldn't handle another argument. Meegan was two; she didn't need to be getting caught up in all that beauty stuff yet. He would discuss it with Isla another time. For now, they were going to enjoy a nice family evening together.

As they sat down to eat that evening, rain began splashing against the windows with a sudden fury; the tension in the air finally lifted.

Chapter Three

Little Miss Southern Star

Aiden took a long drink from his coffee and looked down sadly at his half eaten breakfast, knowing that he was going to have to admit defeat.

'What's wrong?' Isla asked from across the table. 'Don't you like your breakfast?'

'It is wonderful,' he began.

'Don't you feel well?'

'I feel fine.'

'So what is it?'

Aiden hesitated. Isla was getting really prickly about things lately and he didn't want another argument. The truth of it was that every day since moving to Avalon she insisted on cooking him a massive breakfast each morning, 'to build him up for the day,' apparently, but it was just too much. Aiden was used to a liquid breakfast; on the rare occasions that he did eat it was usually just a bagel snatched from a vendor on his dash into work. Being confronted with a plate overflowing with bacon rashers, eggs both scrambled and fried, grits, French toast and beans was starting to make him feel sick. He knew he had to tread gently when expressing his thoughts to Isla; she was just being nice to him after all.

'I don't normally eat a big breakfast, and while it is lovely sometimes, some days, just cereal would do.'

To his relief, Isla just nodded in agreement.

'That's fine, Aid. As long as it isn't because you don't like my cooking or something! It is hard to know when enough is enough. I've never normally cooked for you before and I'm still getting used to my new role. I guess I need to pull back a bit or else you and Meegan are going to become whales!'

He reached out and touched her hand.

'You are doing an amazing job. I had no idea that you had all this in you!'

'Well, you were never around that much before to see.'

'I'm here now and I don't want to miss a thing!' The couple smiled warmly at one another.

'If you are all finished, I'll start clearing up,' Isla began collecting together the various plates and cutlery from the table.

'I'll help,' Aiden offered, rising to his feet,

'No, no, you've got work, let me handle this. Finish your coffee.' Without any further persuasion he sat back down and returned to drinking the jet black stimulant from his favorite blue mug. It was chipped and cracked all over but he loved it. Coffee just didn't taste the same in anything else. He had lost count of the times Isla had tried to throw it out, she thought it tacky and old. But Aiden had developed a strange attachment to his mug. Perhaps it was because it had been a gift from his mother before she had passed away. Whatever the reason, his favorite start to the day was enjoying putting his old mug to his lips and savouring the contents from inside as they slid down the back of his throat.

'Oh,' Isla called to him over the sound of the faucet filling up the sink with soapy water. 'I saw the local priest when I was walking into town with Meegan. Nice man. Father somebody, I don't remember. He was super friendly, not creepy or anything.'

'That's fine, honey.' Aiden noticed that outside the sun was shining and the sky was a dazzling crystal blue. He always felt better about his upcoming day when the sun was shining, often taking it as a good omen of things to come.

'Nice day today, you taking Meegan anywhere?'

'I thought I might drive out of town a bit, pick up some paints.'

'Great idea, you two will enjoy painting the house together!'

'Any colours you would like?'

'I don't mind,' then, looking at his mug, he added, 'a deep blue, like my mug.'

'Ugh,' Isla sighed in disgust. 'That damn mug. Fine, I'll check out the moody blues for you.'

'It is not a moody blue; it is dark like the depths of the ocean.'

'You say dark, I say dull.'

He was about to protest when Isla yelled out in sudden anger, 'Meegan!'

He looked up at his little daughter to see her wearing her Elmo breakfast bowl as a hat, oatmeal all over her head. She was giggling hysterically. Aiden had to stifle a laugh.

'Oh, you can laugh,' Isla said angrily as she removed the bowl and began mopping up the stoney coloured gloop. 'You are not the one who has to clean this mess up! I've already washed her once this morning!'

Meegan was still giggling away.

'No, Meegan. Bad girl!' Her mother scolded. Still the giggles refused to subside. Isla looked over to Aiden for support.

'Breakfast is for eating, Meegs. Not wearing.'

At her father's stern words the little girl's face scrunched up into a ball and her skin began to turn crimson.

'Now look what you have done!' Isla moaned as Aiden braced himself for what was coming next. Meegan let out a huge scream and began wailing at the top of her lungs. Aiden was relieved to be leaving for work, baffled at how something so small could make a sound so immense. Her wails vibrated throughout his body, making his very bones shake.

'I'm sorry, honey, but I have to go now else I'll be late.' Isla just waved her hand at him, not even turning her head as she continued to clean up the mess surrounding Meegan.

'Are you sure you are OK?' He yelled over the screaming.

'I'm fine, just go!' she still didn't look at him.

Aiden lingered in the doorway, knowing from experience that when a woman said that she was feeling fine more often than not she meant the complete opposite. On not hearing the door slam to announce his departure, Isla looked up.

'Go!' she cried again, getting more and more agitated by Meegan's frantic cries. Her eyes said stay but she was telling him to go; confused, Aiden went with the vocal direction and left. He could still hear Meegan as he got into his car and felt a pang of guilt at driving away when she was so distressed. He hoped that everything would be calmer when he got home. He turned out of the driveway and headed back towards Eastham. He was going to visit Brandy again and had a few questions that he wanted answers to.

After the relatively short drive and the maze of corridors and gates, Aiden found himself once again sat before a Perspex pane of glass, looking into the amber eyes of Brandy White. She seemed even smaller than he had remembered, and her skin was so pale it was almost translucent. Her eyes seemed so dark and sunk. It seemed that her spirit was finally crushed and that her body was just fading away.

'How are you doing?' he asked softly.

'Did you manage to see Father West?' Aiden shook his head.

'Oh, please, Mr. Connelly. I am so, so worried about my soul. I need to see him to make things right.'

'So, you are feeling remorse about your husband's death?' this was good, she was finally beginning to show more normal emotions which would help the case flow more easily.

'No,' she replied flatly.

'I just thought...'

'I want to see Father West because I have always gone and made my peace with God every Sunday since I can remember. Call it comfort or whatever, but feeling like I do not have a connection to him, well, I feel truly dreadful.'

Aiden had to admit that she did look dreadful. Today the orange jumpsuit drowned her tiny frame and she seemed to shiver in her seat even though the room, at least on his side, felt far from cold.

'Would you describe yourself as religious, Brandy?'

'Most definitely.'

'Do you not think that God will be angered by what you did to your husband?' he was eager for answers and saw her faith as a way in.

'No, I think he will understand.' Aiden frowned, bemused by her response.

'Brandy?' he locked eyes with her, but not before double checking that the Dictaphone was recording on the table beside him. 'Why did you kill your husband?'

She smiled, not a cynical, wry smile, but a sweet, warm one, as if she were impressed by Aiden's question.

'Mr. Connelly, you are the first person to ask me that. Isn't that strange?'

'That is strange,' he agreed, baffled at why he had failed to ask her that sooner himself.

'When the police came, everybody was shouting, it was chaos. They put the handcuffs on me and just sent me straight here. I was put in a cell on my own; I suppose they think I am dangerous maybe. No one has been to see me. I hear people talking as they walk by, but no one has asked me why. Even when the police made me take a statement, they asked me what happened and that was that. They didn't want to know why.'

'So why did you do it?'

'Well...it...' Brandy suddenly became extremely agitated. Tears welled up in her eyes and her lips began quivering. She wrung her hands together in an attempt to alleviate her anxiety but it did no good. Her body shook like she was sobbing deep within her soul but she barely made a sound.

'Hey, it's OK,' Aiden tried to calm her. Without really knowing what he was doing, he placed his palm upon the glass. The guards watched him intently, unsure of what he was doing.

Brandy understood and placed her hand against his; the glass was cool to the touch but no longer seemed such a huge barrier.

'I am here,' he almost whispered, 'to help you. I know this is hard.' She began to calm down.

'I need to know what happened, and why it happened. Take as long as you need, but you must tell me everything.' She nodded slowly with understanding.

'I remember hearing somebody say once that the beginning is a very good place to start, so that is what I'll do.'

She withdrew into herself for a moment, then taking a deep breath, she began.

'I have lived in Avalon all my life. You couldn't find a nicer town. The sun seems to always shine and most people greet you with a smile and a kind word, at least they used to...

I was raised by my Ma. My Pa had took off long before I was even born. I don't even know his name. Sometimes I wonder if she even knew who he was for sure. We lived in a trailer, out on Clapham Way. I know what you must be thinking, trash, right?'

Aiden shook his head. Brandy bit her lip, unsure whether to carry on.

'Please, continue,' he urged.

'See, lots of folk live in trailers at some point, when times get hard. Without a steady man and a kid in tow, it was all my Ma could afford. I had a nice childhood for the most part. I played with friends; some lived in nice, fancy houses and had nice things. I never brought anybody home, I wasn't ashamed as such, I just didn't want to be judged. Every Sunday Ma dressed me up real nice and we went to church and we fitted in with everyone else. I was happiest there. Life felt normal when we were at church and Ma seemed happy. But I noticed something was wrong when I was around eight. She had just broken up with, I think his name was Jamie, and it had hit her hard. I'm pretty sure she loved him but I think he had a wife as he wasn't around too much but was always talking about one day making us all a real family. When he left she just seemed to give up. At first it was just drinking, but then she turned to drugs.'

Brandy appeared pained by the memories, but seemed determined to carry on.

'Trailer parks don't attract the best people so it was easy for her to get drugs. I'm not sure what she took. She smoked it, used needles, anything. I lost count of the times I would come home from school to find her passed out. I'd have to run to the doctor's house, no matter what time it was, to get help. It got so bad he gave me his home number to call in an emergency, but since we didn't have a phone I never used it. Things got worse and she would often be out of it for days. Often it felt like she didn't even know I was there. I knew she needed help but she wouldn't listen to me and there was no way I was going to leave her. She was all I had.'

Aiden was listening intently but Brandy stopped again.

'Before I carry on, you must promise me something.'

'Sure.'

'You must not pity me, Mr. Connelly. I know I didn't have the best upbringing and a part of me hates my Ma, hates her for not having the strength to cope without a man by her side. But no good ever came of pity. Maybe how things were then is why I'm sitting here today, but I'd rather you left here having learned something than pitying me.'

'It can't have been easy but I don't pity you,' Aiden lied, feeling guilty of how easy and sheltered his own childhood was.

'Sometimes she would make me go collect drugs for her. I didn't realize what was going on at first. Then, as I got older, men started to look at me more. I got breasts and a butt and Ma realized that she could use me as currency to get drugs.'

Aiden felt his breath catch in his throat as he took in what she was saying.

'I've blacked out the worst of it. Thanks to Father West, he helped me make sense of it all. But what with taking care of Ma and everything else, I just stopped going to school. I tried to keep it up as much as I could but, well, I dropped out at fifteen. Of all the things I have done in this life, leaving school is what fills me with the most shame.'

She wiped a stray tear that had fallen down her cheek.

'God is testing us you see. Life is just one big test and I would hate to think that I had failed. At fifteen things looked really bad. I didn't know what I was going to do with my life. That's when Ma found out about the Little Miss Southern Star pageant. The prize money was $10,000. With that kind of money we could buy a house and finally have a proper life. She signed me up and I was really excited. We both were. She started doing my hair pretty and showing me how to wear make-up. I just loved that she was finally taking notice of me and seemed to be drinking less, but looking back, she was only bothering with me because she saw that I could make her some money. Still, she was acting like a mother and I was determined not to let her down.'

'Miss Southern Star is open to girls from all the Southern states aged between 16 and 19. The main competition was just two days after my sixteenth birthday so I only just made it in. The first few rounds went by in a blur. It seemed unreal when I made it to the final. The local paper interviewed me, I became a local celebrity! I was so excited about representing Avalon. My dress was beautiful, pink satin with sequins. The church held a fund-raiser to help pay for my various costumes, but that dress, it just took my breath away. It was by far the nicest thing I had ever owned.'

As she spoke about the competition, the colour returned to Brandy's cheeks and the light within her began to glow again. It was clear to Aiden that this had been a very happy time in her life.

'I was so nervous the day of the finals, I couldn't eat a thing. I threw up twice on the way there! Ma cussed me and said it was important that I kept my nerve. She told me that as long as I got up on that stage and kept smiling that everything would be alright. There were so many people there, it was crazy. I felt so special in my pink gown, with Ma there cheering me on. She had even started to drink less; I think that with the attention we were getting in town she didn't want to ruin it all by her problems coming out. I even started to have this daydream that my Dad would see me in the papers and come find me and make Ma happy again.'

'In the end there were three finalists. I can still remember their names; Andie-Mae Watkins from Georgia. She was so pretty with green eyes and the reddest hair, like fire. And Kaitlin Banks, can't recall where she was from. She had black hair and the whitest skin. She reminded me of Snow White. Then there was little old me. Those two girls were so stunning; I never dreamt that I could possibly win. When they read out my name as the winner I thought that I was going to faint with joy! It was amazing! I can't tell you, Mr. Connelly, just how glorious it felt. It was like every birthday and Christmas at once. They put this gorgeous crown on my head; it was so delicate, made of gold with emerald stones in it. Oh, and the sash. Looking down and seeing Miss Southern Star written across me, well, I broke down and cried. Ma had told me that no matter what, I mustn't cry as I'd ruin my make-up but I couldn't help it. It was just all too wonderful.'

For a moment, Brandy was lost in her memory. Back there on the stage, engulfed in the deafening rumble of applause. A thousand tiny lights sparkled before her, the flash of a camera forever capturing her elation. Then her happiness began to fade once more as the memory gave way to the present.

'I was so amazingly happy. Ma was so proud, I thought that I had it made,' she told Aiden. 'But then...' her voice broke off, wracked with emotion.

'What happened?' Aiden asked softly.

'After I won, the officials wanted documents, you know, to verify everything. I had always failed to produce my high school diploma you see. On account of the fact that I never got it. However, I'd lied on the application. I guess I wanted to enter so bad I never thought that it would matter that I had dropped out of school. I was stupid enough to believe that all they cared about were my looks. But it mattered. It mattered a lot. Apparently I was an unsuitable role model to be Miss Southern Star and because I lied, I was disqualified. They stripped me of my crown, it was the worst moment of my life. The shame, it was unbearable. Everyone in Avalon turned against me, calling me a liar and a cheat. I couldn't walk down the street without people yelling cruel things at me. I wanted to leave but I had nowhere to go.'

'Ma took it worse than everyone else. She started to hate me. She told me I'd ruined the last chance we had at happiness. She stopped talking to me and just drank all day and did drugs all night. She was a mess. I didn't know what to do, in desperation I turned to Father West. I hadn't been to church in a long time; I was too ashamed to face everyone there. But Father West, he reached out to me and offered me kindness that only someone close to God could. I had no choice but to tell him about Ma.'

Brandy held her head in her hands, her fingers digging into her scalp.

'You have to understand, Mr. Connelly, I could not cope with her anymore. She was going to die!'

'I understand, Brandy. So what did Father West do?'

'He took her away. Her problems were so bad that she had to be sectioned. I tried to visit her a couple of times but she always refused to see me. Then, the last time I went, they said she had been discharged. I've no idea where she went. Apparently she met another addict in there and went to live with him. I kept hoping her anger would subside and she would come see me, or at least write, but she never has. I've no idea where she is to this day.'

She sat up again and sighed deeply, her face was pained with regret.

'So it was just me, in the trailer. I got a job at the florist, helping arrange flowers and that. I kept myself to myself. I felt that everyone always kept me at a safe distance, by now everyone knew about Ma's troubles and I think that they assumed I was trouble too. I had no friends, no family. It was a lonely time. I met Brandon just after I'd turned seventeen. I couldn't believe it when he started talking to me. He was the local hero, I felt like the local whore. He was so handsome and popular, he took me to parties and because I was with him people started to talk to me more.'

'Time's up', the guard from the left of Brandy suddenly informed them.

'That is fine,' Aiden began collecting together his things. 'We will continue this another time.'

Brandy nodded sadly, still overcome by the painful emotions of her past.

'Sharing pain does not ease the burden you carry, it just makes others hurt,' she said wistfully as she was being escorted out.

The main church in Avalon stood proud opposite the local hair salon. It was a modest building, the windows were not made from stained glass and the fence around the front had seen better days. It reminded Aiden of a well loved toy, the cracks that appeared on the surface were merely an indication of how much the building was loved and frequented by the people of the town.

It was a beautiful sunny Sunday morning so the family had decided to walk to the church. Isla was wearing a floral sundress which emphasized her beautiful curves, Aiden was in a shirt and khaki pants and Meegan had been allowed to wear one of her Disney princess dresses. She was skipping along merrily, a parent holding each of her little hands. Most people had the same idea as them, it seemed, as numerous families were meandering along the roads, all heading towards the same destination.

Outside the church, the notice board read: 'Trinity Church will be cheering on the Avalon Angels this Wednesday!' Aiden thought it was endearing how the whole town got behind the high school football team.

'We should go,' he nodded at the notice as they walked in.

'To the game?' Isla asked.

'Yeah, I think it would be fun.'

'Sure.'

Inside the church was bustling as the parishioners piled into the wooden pews. Aiden swiftly ushered Isla and Meegan into an empty row at the back; he didn't feel comfortable being up at the front with the more hardcore churchgoers. The wood was stiff and hard beneath his back, reminding him why he hadn't been to church in so long.

Meegan couldn't get settled and climbed up onto her father's lap.

'Whoa, you just get heavier and heavier,' he joked, tickling her sides.

'Make sure she keeps quiet during the service,' Isla hissed. She was taking it all rather seriously.

'Aiden!' A man called from a few rows ahead, waving furiously. He looked up to see Edmond Copes, surrounded by a huge brood of a family. He waved back, as did Meegan. 'We will talk later,' he mouthed to Aiden.

After a few more people had settled in the service began. The church was packed; some late arrivals were forced to stand at the back. It wasn't as formal and dull as Aiden had feared; Father West was an engaging man who had an amazing connection with the people. He looked to be somewhere in his mid forties, with dark curly hair which was showing no sign of turning grey. He had bright blue eyes and stood at an impressive six foot. He was a handsome man for sure. Just to clarify, he whispered to Isla during the service, 'What do you think of Father West?'

'He seems lovely,' she cooed, not even taking her eyes off the priest to answer her husband.

An hour later, when the service had ended, Aiden hung back, wanting to speak with Father West about Brandy. He was lingering outside, Meegan asleep in his arms, when Edmond Copes came ambling over.

'Aiden, my boy, so lovely to see you here. And this must be your darling wife,' he shook Isla's hand. 'A pleasure to meet you, my dear. How are you finding Avalon?'

'Oh, it is really lovely, we are starting to find our feet now.'

'Good, good'. A portly woman with white hair came over. 'Allow me to introduce my wife, Carol,' Aiden politely shook her hand, as did Isla.

'I've been meaning to see you,' she told his wife. 'Knowing that you are new in town, I wondered if you'd like to join my book club...' the two women wandered off, lost in their own chit chat. He watched Isla for a moment, in case she flashed him her 'I need saving' face, but she appeared to be happy in Carol's company.

As Aiden and Edmond stood declaring what a fine day it was, a tall, thin man walked out of the church, some while later than everyone else. Edmond immediately cornered him and shook his hand furiously.

'Aiden, I am pleased to introduce Buck Fern, our local sheriff. Buck, this is my new partner, Aiden Connelly. Came here all the way from Chicago!'

Aiden offered his hand to Buck but he ignored it.

'Pardon my rudeness,' he explained in a slow, Southern drawl which was laced with a slight lisp. 'But until I know a man, I will not shake his hand.' Aiden was put out by his attitude but decided against saying anything; he was, after all, the sheriff. Buck Fern had small slits for eyes and a face ravaged by age. His thinning hair had been strategically combed over but it wasn't fooling anyone. He regarded Aiden with suspicion.

'Ed tells me you are handling the White case?'

'That's right.'

'That wretched whore deserves to burn in hell.' Aiden was shocked at the sheriff's harsh words.

'Buck is always more than happy to assist us with our cases,' Edmond said awkwardly, feeling uncomfortable with Buck's surly behavior.

'Is that so?' Aiden queried the old man, trying to keep his temper in check as he knew he had valuable resources. 'In that case, I need to see the police report from the night of the murder.'

Buck's cheeks flushed and he pursed his small lips in anger. 'Why might that be?'

Aiden was enjoying making the old dinosaur cross. 'Protocol in any murder case. I need to review all the evidence.'

'Protocol?' Buck spat at him. Edmond was looking decidedly uncomfortable and made his excuses and scampered off. The old man stared down Aiden for a moment but he refused to flinch.

'Fine,' the sheriff admitted defeat. 'But be careful, if you shake too many trees, a bee might just come out and sting you,' and with that strange threat Buck Fern ambled off. Aiden was seething after his encounter with the sheriff. He was all riled up and ready to go home and let off some steam when he saw Father West. Isla was now beside him again so he grabbed her arm and walked over to the priest.

'Father?'

50

'Yes, can I help you?' he looked Aiden and Isla over. 'I don't believe that we have met before.'

'I'm Aiden Connelly, this is my wife, Isla, and this lump over my shoulder responds to Meegan when she is awake. We recently moved here.'

'Ahhh yes, you are working with Edmond Copes?' Aiden nodded. 'News travels fast in a town this small. Welcome to Avalon, I hope that you enjoyed the service.'

'Oh, yes, Father, it was wonderful,' Isla told him a little too enthusiastically. He smiled at her warmly.

'Some found it not so interesting,' he nodded at Meegan and laughed.

'Actually,' Aiden passed Meegan to his wife, a not so subtle hint that he wanted to be left alone with Father West. 'I need to talk with you.'

The priest nodded solemnly as Isla reluctantly began walking back to the house, Meegan still sleeping soundly.

Father West led Aiden back inside the cool of the church.

'I'm representing Brandy White,' he began. At the mention of her name Father West seemed pained. 'You were close with her?'

'Yes, I was, she was a very troubled young woman, such a terrible business.'

'Well, she has been asking to see you, over at Eastham. I wondered if you could possibly go and see her.'

Father West nodded slowly. 'No doubt she wants to make peace with God. I will go and see her, that is not a problem. I've known her many years and have been deeply troubled by all that has occurred.'

Aiden found himself lingering, unsure of how to proceed.

'Everyone is quick to judge her,' Father West offered, sensing what was troubling Aiden. 'But I think for someone, as spiritual as she is, to do what she did, well, there must be some form of logic in her mind, don't you think?'

'Yes,' Aiden agreed, wondering if Father West knew more than he was letting on. 'I need to find out more about the case as a whole. Brandon appears to be very loved around here.'

'Oh, yes, indeed.' Aiden didn't want to press Father West for any more information, it didn't seem right, especially in a church. He was about to leave when the priest called after him;

'Tread carefully, Mr. Connelly.' Aiden nodded solemnly and turned to walk home, even more sure that there was much more to this case than meets the eye.

Chapter Four

He's Our Hero

Brandon White – Our Shining Knight was the headline. Aiden Connelly was sat in a library, scouring old newspapers for stories about Brandon White. His high school football career had been heavily documented by the local paper, the Avalon Informer, and when his team won the state championship he appeared in even more publications. In each article he was hailed as a true team player, who was not lacking in courage or passion. The numerous pictures showed that he was strikingly handsome; he had a chiselled jaw and a deep tan with soft blue eyes. Aiden learned that, like Brandy, he had lived in Avalon all his life, yet his childhood had been a much more stable one. His father owned a successful local company, Avalon Pine, where Brandon later went to work after graduating from high school. He was six foot two and well built, once again highlighting Aiden's confusion as to how Brandy had managed to overpower him. In the brief police report that Edmond had given to him there had been no record of toxins in his blood which means that he can't have been drunk.

He read how Brandon had taken his high school football team, the now famous Avalon Angels, to win their first ever state championship almost ten years ago. It was the first time they had won such a prestigious award and his success has yet to be repeated, which undoubtedly had helped cement his reputation as a local saviour.

Aiden had been disturbed by his encounters with Buck Fern and Father West at church, so the following dawn he had driven out of town to a college library to gather some sources and find out more about the enigma that was Brandon White. In every interview he gave he was polite and well spoken, constantly praised for his gentlemanly manner. It was getting increasingly difficult to understand why Brandy would have killed him.

As Aiden scanned through the papers, he came across an excerpt marking their wedding day. He did the math, Brandy was a young bride at 19 and Brandon was 23. That was five years ago. In the small photograph the couple are beaming happily and seem the picture of wedded bliss. The byline described how, 'local football hero marries former beauty queen.' The reference to Brandy's shambolic time as Miss Southern Star surprised him, perhaps even not enough time had passed by the time she wed for the bad blood over her disqualification to have been forgiven.

The final entry for Brandon White was his obituary. It was a glowing review of a young man who loved his family, served his community and basically never put a foot wrong. Brandy was sparsely mentioned, only in the conclusion, when she was named as the prime suspect for his murder. Having been married for five years, Aiden wondered if those closest to the couple had ever sensed that something was wrong. There would be no point in tracking down Brandy's mother as she would not even be aware that her daughter had been married. Clyde White seemed like a good source. He was Brandon's father and from the articles Aiden deemed that they were very close. Perhaps he could shed some light on his son's marriage.

Once he felt he had successfully found all the articles relating to Brandon, Aiden turned his attention to Brandy, in particular the Miss Southern Star competition. A small voice in his head queried if she was being entirely honest with him and he wanted to silence it.

When Brandy had said that the whole town had turned against her she wasn't exaggerating. At first the Avalon Informer had championed its young beauty queen; from the moment she made it past the preliminary rounds she was receiving a mention within the front pages, and when she won a photograph of her smiling proudly made the front page. The paper gushed about how she was a sweet local girl done good; there was no mention that she lived in a trailer or of her mother's troubles. However, all that changed once news broke of her disqualification.

Little Miss Scheming Star was one of the kinder headlines. Her controversial stripping of the crown even made national papers. They called her trailer trash, mocked her mother's addictions and said that she had brought shame upon Avalon. She then disappeared off the radar, her name only appearing once she was connected to Brandon. Considering she was made a local hate figure, people must have wondered what Brandon saw in her. She was stunningly beautiful, but having the reputation that he did, he must have been able to have any girl he wanted.

Aiden sat there pondering on it all. He realized that he needed to press Brandy further for answers. He felt relieved that thus far she had told him the truth. It was always so much easier to represent a client when you felt that you could trust them.

Seated in his car, before he started his engine to travel back to Avalon, Aiden pulled out his mobile phone. He called Eastham to inform them that he would be visiting Brandy again the following day. Then he called Betty to inform her that he wouldn't be in until the afternoon; Edmond was also out of the office working. Finally, he dialed Avalon Pine from the number he had sourced on the Internet moments earlier; a pleasant woman informed him that Clyde White would be on site all day. Aiden turned the key in the ignition and set off to pay Brandon's father a visit.

Avalon Pine was located on the outskirts of town. Aiden parked in the designated customer lot and walked over to what he presumed were the offices; a long log cabin with the company logo emblazoned on the side. Inside the wooden structure it was blissfully cool, thanks to half a dozen fans whirring away. It was an insanely hot day, Aiden was thankful that his car had air conditioning. In Chicago, air conditioning came as standard wherever you went, but in Avalon, things were different. Only the well-to-do could afford such a commodity; most people made do with electric fans scattered around the place, as was the case with the offices at Avalon Pine.

A heavily made-up young blonde woman was seated behind an ample desk filing away at her nails. She greeted him with the fakest smile he had ever seen, her lips a most unnatural shade of fluorescent pink.

'I'm looking for Clyde White,' he told her.

'Is Mr. White expecting you? She asked insincerely, obviously not really caring what answer he gave.

'No, but if he has five minutes I'd really like to talk to him, it's regarding the trial of Brandy White.' The false lashes framing her eyes widened in interest. She was suddenly much more attentive, realizing that she was witnessing some potentially high level gossip.

'Please, take a seat and I'll call him, Mr…'

'Connelly.' Aiden settled himself down on a pine bench in the lobby area, watching as her lacquered nails furiously clicked numbers into the phone on her desk.

'Mr. White, sorry to disturb you, I have a Mr. Connelly here to see you,'

Aiden was too far away to be able to hear Clyde's response. The receptionist lowered her tone.

'I think it is something to do with Brandon, he must be a lawyer or something.' More silence as she nodded whilst her boss responded. At last she put the phone down and flashed her Barbie smile at Aiden once again.

'He says that you can go right through. His office is just across the lumber yard, you can't miss it.' Aiden thanked her and stepped back out into the heat; he was beginning to thoroughly regret wearing a suit.

Avalon Pine was clearly a successful business. The lumber yard was bustling, as various burly men in T-shirts and jeans carried huge planks of wood here and there. Aiden could make out what appeared to be a warehouse; the huge open doors revealed garden sheds in various stages of production. Across the large yard was another pine log cabin, identical to the one he had just been in. As he got closer he could make out the sign on the door: Clyde White, Site Manager. He knocked twice.

'Come in,' came a voice from within. Aiden pushed open the door and was greeted with refreshing cold air, yet there were no fans in sight; this was an air-conditioned building, another indication of Clyde White's success.

Inside there was a large desk, with two leather chairs opposite it; the walls were lined with framed photographs and newspaper clippings. Aiden immediately recognized Brandon in a number of them.

Clyde White was immaculately dressed. He wore a crisp white shirt and grey trousers, his black hair was streaked with silver and his face was heavily lined, yet he was strikingly handsome. He was what Isla would refer to as a 'silver fox', meaning that he was a very attractive older man. Beneath the shirt, it was clear that he was in good shape. Aiden felt slightly intimated as he held out his hand and introduced himself.

'Do take a seat,' Clyde instructed him. He had the same chiseled jaw and pale blue eyes as his son.

'Thank you for agreeing to see me,' Aiden began. 'I work for Cope and May Attorneys at Law, I am currently representing Brandy White, and as part of my investigations into the case, I am eager to learn more about your son, Brandon.' At the mention of his son, Clyde White seemed to age ten years.

'That is, only if it is not too painful to talk about,' Aiden added, starting to wonder if it had been a bad idea to come and see Mr. White.

'No, Mr. Connelly, I am always more than happy to talk about my son. He was a truly wonderful young man, an inspiration.'

'Of course'. Father West's cryptic warning to tread carefully lingered in his mind. He knew that if he was going to get any useful information about Brandon from his father he needed to gain his trust first.

'I've read about his triumphant days on his school football team.' Clyde smiled proudly at this. 'Did he ever think about going pro?'

Clyde leaned back in his chair, thinking hard. 'He had the talent, no doubt about that, but he loved his family too much to leave. The good teams, where you could make a career out of playing, were all too far away.'

'So he worked here?'

'Sure did. He was my right-hand man; and the hardest worker I ever knew. All the guys loved him, I'd hoped that one day he would take over the business for me but now…' Clyde gazed at his desk in sadness. 'He was my only son, my only child.'

Any preconceived theories that Aiden had once had were slipping away. Clyde White was shaken to the core over the death of his son whom he had loved dearly. If Brandon was at all like his father, well spoken, intelligent, it was making it even harder to identify a motive for Brandy to have killed him. He knew that he had to dig deeper.

'What did you think of Brandy?' Clyde's face suddenly distorted with disgust.

'Little tramp. Blinded my son with her 'butter wouldn't melt' face and then…' Aiden noticed that his fists were now clenched tightly in anger.

'They were together a long time before it happened. Five years. How did she and Brandon get along?'

'Fine, they seemed in love. She never came down to the yard when he was working so I didn't see all that much of her, except the odd weekend when they came over for lunch and on the holidays. She was always polite, bit too quiet really. She never said much; it was clear Brandon didn't marry her for her brains.'

As discreetly as possible, Aiden switched on the Dictaphone which was concealed in his jacket pocket. Clyde's perception of Brandy could prove invaluable later on in court.

'She had a rather unconventional upbringing,' he said, trying not to sound too sensitive towards Brandy.

'Oh yeah, her mother was a whack job. Whole town knew about her troubles. And then that whole beauty pageant thing.

58

We weren't happy when Brandon started knocking about with her, to say the least.'

'What else was Brandon interested in, besides football?'

'The usual, hanging with guys, watching sports, movies. He never read books or anything, his grades were average. His talents lay in the more physical aspects of things.'

'So he didn't gamble or drink excessively?'

'No!' Clyde White snapped. 'My son was a gentleman through and through.'

'I only asked as I'm trying to ascertain a motive for his murder. I didn't know your son, but what I can gather from the people of Avalon is that he was a great man.'

'The greatest.'

'So it must have been one hell of a shock when Brandy murdered him.'

'Truly shocking,' Clyde agreed, but something in his eyes gave him away. Was it regret, sadness? Aiden could not tell so he tried to push him further;

'Do you have any idea what may have driven her to do it?'

'None at all. Isn't it your job to find out why she did it? She is probably as crazy as her jacked up mother. It wouldn't surprise me if she had been high as a kite for years.'

'Well, I sincerely hope to get to the bottom of it all.'

'As long as that little witch pays for what she has done,' Clyde's voice shook with emotion, his eyes narrowed in spite.

'Do you know if Brandy had any friends in town, anyone I could talk to?' Clyde shook his head.

'That girl was all about Brandon. Once they got married she stopped working and just stayed home. She was always at church though, seemed quite friendly with Father West, but then he was the one who had sent her mother away.' Clyde glanced at his watch and seemed anxious.

'I am very sorry, Mr. Connelly but I have got work to attend to.'

'Well, thank you very much for your time.' Both men rose to their feet and shook hands.

'If I can be of any further help, do not hesitate to call,' Clyde handed him a business card.

'I won't.' Aiden had one hand on the door handle and was about to leave when Clyde called him back.

'One more thing, this Wednesday, it is a big game for the Avalon Angels. You should really try and come. That team meant everything to Brandon, thought you might want to check it out.'

'Yes, I will, always been a big football fan anyway.'

'Oh yeah, who is your team?'

'Chicago Bears.'

'Awww no, Dallas Cowboys all the way. I never miss a game!' Clyde smiled and waved goodbye.

Outside and back in the heat Aiden felt no more closer to finding the truth; if anything he felt that he was edging further away from it. He needed to talk to Brandy again as soon as possible.

Betty was sat at her desk, two fans billowing air at her, her normally immaculate hair dishevelled and soaked with sweat.

'Too hot for you, Betty?'

'Oh, I have always struggled with the heat. Ever since I was a girl. And these damn fans do nothing, they just circulate warm air! Edmond has said that I can leave as soon as all the admin for today is sorted. I honestly don't know why he doesn't just get air conditioning like everybody else!' Her cheeks were flushed and she seemed extremely agitated. Aiden decided against asking her for a coffee.

In the main office Edmond was looking equally flustered in the heat. There were fans on in the room but none were directed at him; they would cause havoc on the mounds of paperwork scattered around. He was sweating profusely as he typed away on his keyboard.

'Aiden, my boy, how are you holding up in this weather? It is not normally this hot in Avalon!'

Aiden undid the top few buttons of his shirt but they offered little comfort from the stifling heat. The air outside was so still, there wasn't even the slightest breeze; it was unbearable.

'All this mounting heat is no good,' Edmond moaned. 'There will be one hell of a storm soon, that's for sure.' The air in Avalon was indeed electric; you didn't need to be a weatherman to know that some turbulent weather was heading their way.

'Hope it comes before Wednesday. The boys can't play good football in this damned heat!'

'Speaking of football,' Aiden was already typing away on his computer, writing up his conclusions from his encounter with Clyde. 'You follow the Dallas Cowboys?'

'Sure do, son. Think everyone around here does. Why you ask?'

'I went to see Clyde White before and he mentioned it. Figured Avalon was pretty big on sport, what with all the support the Angels get and that.'

'You went to see Clyde?' Edmond asked curiously.

'Yeah, I'm trying to piece together an idea of what Brandon White was like. No one says a bad word against him.'

'Well, people aren't going to speak ill of the dead.'

Aiden looked over at Edmond in surprise. 'So, you think if he weren't dead people's opinion of him would be different?'

'No, no,' Edmond was sweating even more. Was it the heat or was he feeling suddenly under pressure? 'It is just an expression. Folks around here have always loved Brandon.'

'Oh, I get that. The sheriff, Buck Fern wasn't it? He seems...' Aiden struggled to find the right word. 'Protective, of Brandon.'

'Old Buck can be like that. I'm sorry if he came across as rude yesterday. He just isn't the social type, never has been. I'm sure that once he gets to know you he will be as nice as pie.' Aiden doubted that somehow.

'So how was Clyde holding up? I keep meaning to go over and see him but I've been bogged down with work lately. Once the Brandy White case is all sorted I'm afraid I've got a nice pile of divorce proceedings I could really use your help with.'

'Can't wait,' Aiden laughed sarcastically. 'Clyde White seems like a genuine guy. Got a nice set-up with his company. Losing his son must have hit him real hard.'

'He's not been the same since,' Edmond noted softly. 'Always been such a composed man though. Takes himself very seriously as a businessman. I don't think he is all that comfortable with the scandal of it all. He hasn't been to church in a long while, probably isn't up to facing the whole town yet, but you would think he would want to find some solace in God. Who knows?'

'Mr. Copes,' Betty's voice was disjointed through the intercom.

'Yes, Betty?'

'I really cannot stand this heat any longer. I'm afraid I've got to clock off. I'll be in all the earlier tomorrow to make up for lost time.'

'Don't be silly, Betty, my love. Go home and have some iced tea and come in usual time tomorrow.'

'Thank you, Mr. Copes. Goodnight, and goodnight to Mr. Connelly, too.' A few moments later the two men heard the soft whisper of chimes as Betty left for a cooler climate.

'This heat is utterly ridiculous, poor old girl. I think it is worse for her, because, you know, she is going through that phase.'

'Phase?' Aiden was confused.

'You know,' Edmond seemed embarrassed by what he was trying to convey to his younger colleague. 'They call it, 'the change.''

'Oh,' Aiden felt his face flush. Why do men always fall apart at the mere mention of female problems? Every time Isla was on her period Aiden felt like an awkward twelve year old all over again. He hated it when she used to ask him to pick up tampons at the store, and he always got the wrong ones as in his haste he never read the labels properly. When she said words to him like, 'heavy flow,' he would just shut down and try to blank it all out. You would think he would have the maturity to deal with it all, but as Edmond had proved, men fail to grow out of their awkwardness with the female anatomy.

'I suppose we should head home too,' Edmond sighed, succumbing to the intensifying heat. 'I think I am beginning to melt into this chair,' he peeled himself up from the leather seat which was now soaked in his sweat.

'I'm going to battle it out a bit longer. I need to get some paperwork sorted. I'm heading to Eastham again tomorrow.'

'Ah, right. Well I'll leave you with the keys then. Which reminds me, I need to get Betty to cut you your own set. We both have one, makes sense that you do too. Just in case you ever get the urge to come into the office at ungodly hours, not that I ever do, but there you go,' he tossed a set of brass keys on a Dallas Cowboys keychain over to Aiden.

'Just drop them off on your way home tomorrow.'

'Thanks, I will.'

'And don't work too late!' Edmond called as he retreated to the sanctuary of his air-conditioned car.

Aiden was lost in his own world as he wrote up reams of notes and scoured the Internet for as much information as he could find. As he had suspected, Avalon Pine was a long established company which had enjoyed moderate success over the years. He needed to get Brandy to open up about her marriage with Brandon. He was definitely missing some pieces of the puzzle and he felt that a majority of them lay with her. When Aiden glanced up at the clock it was 6:30pm.

'Dammit,' he muttered angrily, hastily switching off his computer and gathering his things together. He was late for dinner and he knew that Isla would not be happy.

'You're late,' Isla snapped before he had chance to even come through the door.

'I know, I know,' Aiden held his hands up defensively. 'I was busy at work and I lost track of time.' His wife's face was set in a harsh glare, her arms folded across her chest. He could tell that she was in the mood for an argument, but feeling tired and hot, all he wanted to do was relax with an ice cold beer.

'I thought the whole point of being here was that you didn't have to work late!'

'It was…it is. I just got caught up with stuff. Isla, I'm sorry, it won't happen again,' he was happy to admit defeat and say whatever she wanted in order to diffuse the situation quickly.

'Fine,' she sighed. 'I fed Meegan but put our dinners in the oven.' Aiden watched as she removed a whole pizza from the oven. He unbuttoned his shirt nearly half way down and helped himself to a beer from the fridge. The cool glass felt like heaven in his hands, and when the amber liquid slid down his dry throat he felt himself reach a euphoric state of ecstasy.

'Ah,' he gasped in satisfaction.

'You know, I slaved over dinner.'

'Babe, it's a pepperoni pizza, which I doubt you made from scratch.'

Isla was chomping through her first slice and replied to him whilst still chewing; 'No, but still, I had to heat it, and make Meegan her dinner.'

Aiden just nodded and began to eat the meal that had been so lovingly prepared for him.

Two bottles of beer and half a pizza later, Aiden was feeling flushed with contentment. He was sprawled out on the couch watching a baseball match on the television through drooping eyes.

'Daddy!' Meegan came running in and bounced on his chest.

'Owww,' he cried in protest as she began using him as a human trampoline. 'Get off Daddy!'

After a few more jumps she obeyed. She was wearing a bright pink nightdress and from the minty smell on her breath had just brushed her teeth and so was all ready for bed.

'Will you read me a bedtime story?'

'Sure thing, princess.' He groggily sat up and shook his head in an attempt to wake up. 'Where's Mommy?'

'Right here,' Isla came down the stairs. She still seemed to be annoyed with Aiden so he had been doing his best to avoid her until she calmed down.

'I had a bath!' Meegan told her Dad proudly.

'Good girl, at least you don't smell then.'

'Come on,' she was tugging on his hand, leading him towards the staircase.

'OK, OK, I'm coming.'

'Aid, I was thinking we could watch a movie or something,' Isla grabbed on to his arms, her fingertips gently caressing the soft skin on the underside of his elbows, letting him know what she really meant.

'Honey, I'm pretty beat.' She immediately let go of him and stormed off into the kitchen. Aiden sighed in frustration and followed Meegan upstairs, thankful for the temporary distraction from yet another disagreement with his wife.

He stood and watched Meegan sleeping for a while. She looked so angelic and peaceful. She had only made it up until Snow White meets the dwarfs in the woods when her eyelids grew too heavy and she slipped into that beautiful, dreamless serenity of sleep that only the innocence of youth can bring.

Downstairs Aiden could hear cupboards banging; Isla was clearly still mad. Her immature attitude really grated on him sometimes. Meegan was trying to sleep yet she was still childishly making a commotion to get his attention. As much as he just wanted to ignore her and get to bed himself, he could not risk her waking their daughter so he went downstairs to face the fire.

'Oh, here you are,' she said nastily, placing the remains of the night's dishes into the appropriate cupboards.

'I'm sorry I worked late.'

'I know you are.'

'Then what's wrong?'

She sat down at the table and looked up at him with sad eyes.

'I'm worried you are not attracted to me anymore.'

'Don't be silly,' he reached out to stroke her cheek but she pushed him away.

'I'm not being silly, we used to do it all the time and now...'

'Now, we have a little girl to think about,' Aiden sat down opposite her and held her hands in his. 'Isla, you are beautiful! You know how attracted I am to you.' She began to smile and her anger seemed to be subsiding. As usual, Aiden found that complimenting her was the best way to get her to calm down.

'When you were home late, and then when you blew me off, it just felt like we were slipping back into our old ways and I don't want that.'

'I don't want that either. And we are not. Tonight was a one off, I swear. This case is just bigger than I thought, that's all.'

'Bigger? I thought it was an open, shut case?'

Aiden ran his hands through his hair, he wasn't in the right frame of mind to start discussing the case; he just wanted to switch off for the night. He went to the fridge to get another beer, hoping to avoid her questions.

'Want one?' He asked from the welcoming cool of the open fridge door. Isla nodded so he grabbed a second bottle and handed it to her.

'Aid, the case, why is it bigger than you thought?'

'I don't know, honey,' he took a deep, long swig from his bottle. 'It is a murder case, sure as hell. But I don't get why she did it.'

'Could it be what the French call a 'crime of passion'?'

'I suppose...perhaps,' Aiden thought it over.

'Maybe the husband was having an affair.'

'It's a possibility. I just need to do some more digging around. I'm heading to the prison tomorrow.'

'Again?!'

'Yes, again, I need to ask her a few more questions.'

'What else can she say apart from, 'I'm guilty'?'

'It is more complicated than that.'

'Complicated how?'

'Why don't we go upstairs?' Aiden asked suggestively, not wanting to discuss things further.

'I thought you were tired?' Isla giggled excitedly.

'Yes, but seeing you there, well, you are a beautiful woman, Mrs. Connelly and I'm a lucky, lucky man.'

'Oh, yes you are!' She took his hand and Aiden was once more led up the stairs by a female, only this time he hoped he would be able to make it to the end of the story with her.

Chapter Five

It Will Be All White

Despite the raging heat outside, within the walls of Eastham prison it was eerily cool. Brandy was sat across from him; he wondered if on her side of the Perspex glass the temperature was even colder as she shivered intermittently as they talked.

'I went to church on Sunday and spoke with Father West,' he informed her.

'He is such a truly kind man,' she cooed. Aiden was impressed at the priest's apparent ability to woo women.

'He has said that he will try and come and see you,' at this news Brandy broke into a beaming smile, showing Aiden exactly how she could have originally been crowned Miss Southern Star.

'That is wonderful, thank you so, so much, Mr. Connelly'. In spite of himself Aiden felt himself blushing at her gratitude.

'It is no problem, Brandy, just doing my job.' He hesitated before continuing. He needed to gain more insight into her relationship with Brandon but knew he had to go about it carefully. She had led a tumultuous life and he reasoned that life as a married woman had been no different.

'So, last time we spoke we got up to the point where you met Brandon,'

'Uh huh,'

'Can I ask how you met?'

'Sure. That day is burned in my memory. I can still see him now, clear as day. At school I had grown up knowing all about his football glory. Heck, I'd even been there to cheer him on some games when I was younger! He always looked so handsome and dashing, all the girls went crazy for him. I think he used to date a couple of cheerleaders back in high school, only the prettiest, of course. After school he would knock around town with his friends, cruise down the high street on Friday nights, hang out and drink beer, typical guy stuff. I'd seen him around before, Avalon is a small town, sooner or later you get to see just about everybody. I've never been all that confident with men, I mostly just walked around looking at the floor, didn't want no attention. But after winning Little Miss Southern Star, even though they had taken my crown away and Ma was gone, some days I felt like I was still wearing it. In my mind, I pretended that I was still a winner and would walk around and hold my head high! It was on one of these days that Brandon started talking to me,' she giggled girlishly and blushed.

'I feel like such a fool, telling you this story, Mr. Connelly. You must surely think I'm just a stupid girl'.

'No, of course not, Brandy. What did Brandon say to you?'

'He said', Brandy deepened her voice in an attempt to sound masculine which Aiden found humorous, 'hey, aren't you that beauty girl, Brandy Cotton? I've seen you around.' Then her voice returned to normal.

'Cotton was my maiden name.' Aiden nodded although he was already aware of that. He had searched tirelessly for her mother, Janice Cotton, but to no avail.

'He asked me if I wanted to hang out with him and the guys. Of course I said yes. He was the most handsome guy I'd ever seen. At first there was always a group of us, then we started to be alone more, sometimes even driving to the next town over to catch a movie, and things just sort of, you know, developed.'

'You fell in love?'

'Yes, I did. And it was wonderful. Love is such an amazing thing, it is easy to see why so many people sing and write about it. I cared about Brandon more than anything.' Aiden was touched by her romantic outlook.

'So you two became serious quite quickly?'

'Well,' she bit her lip as she debated how to carry on. 'We went steady for like two years before he proposed. I think that we were both too young to rush things, but by then we knew, it was the real thing. He treated me like an absolute princess, taking me out to fancy restaurants, buying me gifts. It was like being crowned Miss Southern Star on a daily basis! One time, he turned up at the trailer at 3am, with a dozen red roses, saying he couldn't sleep because he missed me so much, and that he had driven 80 miles to find a 24-hour store, just to get me flowers to show me just how much he cared. Isn't that just a wonderful thing to do?'

'Yes, it is.'

'Mr. Connelly, what is the most romantic thing you have done?' Aiden was about to answer and then stopped himself, he didn't want to get too close to Brandy; sharing information about himself could mislead her into thinking that they were friends. Although he needed her to confide in him, so perhaps he needed to open up a bit about himself in order for her to reveal more.

'Well,' he began thinking out loud. 'I guess...' he was shocked to find that he was struggling to think of an answer. In the early haze of dating, he had been hot and heavy with Isla, often opting to stay in and go at it like animals rather than go out. When he met her she wasn't the kind of girl who needed wining and dining. His proposal had been more out of necessity than love; she thought that she was pregnant and his parents pressured him to do the right thing. It turned out to be a false alarm, but he knew the right thing to do was to carry on with the engagement and get married. The pregnancy scare had been the push he needed, at least that's what he told himself. He asked her one morning over breakfast, the way someone might enquire about the weather. Despite the poor delivery Isla had been delighted. Six months later they wed on a yacht at dusk, it was a beautiful ceremony. At twenty four he wondered if he had been too young to wed. He would have been a year older than Brandon was. Two years later, Meegan joined them.

'I once wrote a girl a poem and then sung it to her, to the tune of her favorite song,' as he told her his heart panged when he realized that this was something he did in high school and not for Isla.

'That is really sweet,' Brandy smiled. 'What was the song?' Aiden laughed as he thought back.

'It was Wake Me Up Before You Go Go, by Wham!' They both laughed at this. Her entire face lit up when she laughed; it was almost magical to watch.

'Well, like I said, Brandon could be quite the romantic when he wanted to be. One night there was a raging thunderstorm, I hate storms. I hate them so bad. I saw lightning strike a trailer when I was younger and it caught on fire and killed the people in it who were sleeping. It was the worst thing I'd ever seen. Now every time I hear thunder my blood runs cold. Like today, I know a storm is coming, I can feel it in the air, and even locked away in here I know I'll be scared. So this storm was raging, and I was sat in the trailer on my own, terrified, when Brandon came knocking at the door, soaked to the skin. He said he had been out drinking with the guys but when he heard thunder he knew he had to get to me, to protect me. The rain had come whilst he was running over. He had risked his life to be by my side, and I told him that my life was his, that I wanted to give myself to him forever. He got down on one knee and took off his class ring and handed it to me, saying that he wanted to hold me to that promise and make me his wife. It was such a beautiful moment.'

'Sounds like he was a good husband.'

'No, he was a good boyfriend, a great boyfriend. But people change.'

'What happened?'

'Well, first of all, we got married.'

'Brandon's family were well off. His Dad owns a big pine company, where Brandon also worked and they had a gorgeous big house. When I first went round, I couldn't believe how beautiful it was. I felt so ashamed of my trailer and my Ma, but his family welcomed me in as one of their own. Mrs. White helped me arrange all the wedding, she was brilliant. She booked the venue, invited all the guests, helped me choose my wedding dress, and they paid for everything.'

'Once we had set a date, I tried desperately to find my Ma. I wanted her there more than anything, I wanted her to be proud of me again, but she was long gone. As it drew closer I was so wrapped up in flowers, cake, favors and gift listings that I grew less and less bothered by the fact that my Ma wouldn't be there.'

'Father West performed the service for us, it was so gorgeous. The church was decked out in white ribbons and red roses; it looked like something straight out of a fairy tale. I arrived in a limousine, I felt like a celebrity! Brandon's father, Clyde, gave me away. It felt right after how good he had been to me.'

Aiden recalled how Clyde White had stated that he and his wife weren't happy when Brandon started dating Brandy. Perhaps they had finally warmed to her by the time the young couple were due to wed, although when he had spoken to him, Clyde had only hate for his daughter-in-law, which, under the circumstances, was understandable.

'So, you had a good relationship with Brandon's parents?'
'Oh, the best. We used to be there all the time. But after we got married, we got our own place and we stopped visiting so much.'

'Everyone from town was there,' she was still recollecting her wedding day, a blissful smile on her face.
'Brandon was so popular, and people seemed to have forgotten, or at least forgiven me about Miss Southern Star. I had my hair done up and a wonderful dress. Pure white, and mark my words, Mr. Connelly, I had every right to wear white. Not like some girls, no sir, I had saved myself. At least, you know, with Brandon. Back in the trailer park, when Ma had gotten real bad, things had happened... But I'd moved on from that. I wanted our wedding night to be special, I wanted to do everything right!'

'After the service we went back to Brandon's house, there was a massive marquee in the garden where we were having the reception. We had a band and everything! It was the talk of the town for weeks after. Sheriff Fern even said it was the most wonderful wedding he had ever attended. I felt like a princess, it was almost as good as when I won my title, if my Ma had been there it would easily have been better. But I missed her. Brandon had so many people there for him, his family, friends, Co-workers. I had no one. It hurt like hell when the photographer took pictures with his family and then quietly asked where mine were. But I told him, 'This is my family now.' And that was how I felt, that I finally had a proper family now. Marrying Brandon felt right, and I loved him so much I used to worry that I might burst!'

She was still smiling but there was a sadness in her eyes, still she continued.

'Our first dance was to the Buddy Holly song, True Love Ways. Brandon didn't want that, he had fought me tooth and nail right up until the very last moment. He wanted Always by Bon Jovi, but I'm not much a fan of rock music. I was so surprised when Buddy Holly came on. To me, it just proved how much Brandon cared about me, that he was willing to let me have my song over his. Becoming Mrs. White was truly wonderful, in every sense. He gave me the wedding of my dreams, and in exchange I gave him myself, unconditionally. Which I guess is what marriage is.'

'I suppose,' Aiden agreed. 'Although, you shouldn't lose sight of the person you are, else it affects the marriage.'

'Maybe that is where we went wrong, we lost sight of ourselves. We changed.'

'How did you change?'

'Well,' Brandy's smile was now entirely gone, replaced with a face shrouded in sadness. Grief was clearly weighing heavily on her mind as she contemplated on how to continue.

'As I said, we got our own house. Lovely little place, two bedrooms, one bathroom, a porch and huge lawn out at the back. On a clear day you could sit out and see for miles. Our house was just outside town, all alone except for the Allens' place two miles down the road to the east. I wasn't all too happy about living a bit out like that. I was used to living alone but not being completely alone, there was always people about in the trailer park. There was never complete silence. But out in my house, you could honestly have heard a pin drop some days when there was no breeze. It could be quite creepy, especially at night. Brandon didn't mind where it was, he could drive and had to work most days. But me, I couldn't drive and I didn't know anyone who I could ask to pick me up and take me places. I had to rely on Brandon whenever I wanted to go anywhere.'

'So, the dynamic of the relationship changed?'

'Not right away, but slowly, as more and more time passed he got more and more annoyed about things. Some nights he went out with the guys and wouldn't return home until the following day. I did wonder if perhaps he was cheating on me, but I was giving him what he wanted in the bedroom so he had no reason to stray.'

'I cooked his meals for him; on the table at 6pm sharp for when he got in from work. I washed his clothes, cleaned the house. I did everything but it was so lonely. I asked him time and again for a dog to keep me company but he was having none of it. He stopped treating like a princess; I guess he started taking me for granted. But he began to change, after our first anniversary Brandon was gone, and what I was left with for a husband I grew to hate.'

'Is that what drove you to kill him, your hatred for the man he had become?'

'In part.'

Aiden knew all too well the changes that people undergo once they enter into marriage. He and Isla had practically become strangers in Chicago, occasionally passing like ships in the night as they went about their lives. He had even started to feel estranged from Meegan as he worked longer and longer hours, and to be distant from his own child he could not bear. One day he came home from work and when he took her in his arms she balled her eyes out, as if she did not recognize him. That was the last straw; Aiden knew that if he didn't move his family away from the city they would ultimately be destroyed. He sympathized with Brandy, although he knew not to tell her so.

'Brandon took to drinking a lot. Or so I thought. The more time I lived as his wife, the more I realized how I had never known him at all. He had shown me just one face while we were dating, now I was being introduced to a host of others, and some of them terrified me. He had a drinking problem and it was nothing new. Even at the wedding, he drank so much that when he took me to our marital bed to, you know, do it, he just passed out. He awoke two hours later being sick everywhere. He threw up on my dress, it was terrible. The Brandon I knew would have been ashamed by his behavior, but the next day he wasn't sorry. He even shouted at me for insisting that he pay for my dress to be dry-cleaned! The day I became Mrs. White everything changed, and not for the good.'

Brandy hugged herself with her arms and rested her head on her chest. Aiden noted that they didn't have long left before he would have to leave. They were making good progress but he needed to know more. All marriages have their problems, yet he found it hard to believe that she murdered her husband because he had a drinking problem. There was something else.

'He had a temper,' she said it so quietly, that through the Perspex glass Aiden could hardly hear her.
'Was he violent?' Tears were now running down her cheeks.
'Can I trust you, Mr. Connelly?'
'Yes, of course.'
'Because…everyone loves Brandon…' she was sobbing. 'They don't listen to me…they just looked away and let him…'
Brandy broke down and cried so hard her tiny body shook. Distressed, Aiden pressed his palm to the glass. Through her cries she recognized the gesture, what he was trying to convey to her, shakily she pressed her hand against his and the sobs slowly began to subside.
'He did terrible things,' she whispered.
'Brandy, you need to tell me what he did.' She looked at Aiden through her watery eyes and slowly lifted up the orange sleeves of her jumpsuit to reveal her arms. They were slender and white, but they made Aiden grimace in horror. The perfect

74

white of her skin was littered with scars, a majority appeared to be cigarette burns, but there were also cuts. She quickly pulled her sleeves back down in shame.

'They don't look so bad these days.'

'He did that to you?'

'He did much more than that.' Aiden wanted to ask more but the guards were moving forward to usher her away. He watched her leave, dumbfounded. The local hero, Avalon's Saint, had cruelly beaten his wife, to what extent was currently unclear, and in order to save herself, she had killed him, yet she was the villain. A shiver ran down his spine as he realized that he may no longer be dealing with a murder case; he would just need more proof to back up Brandy's allegations. He would also need to get her to confess to exactly what he did to her, no matter how awful.

His skin was soaked in sweat before he had even got to his car. The heat was ridiculous. Grey clouds hung ominously on the horizon. Aiden began his drive home, his mind awash with broken heroes and tortured beauty queens.

Isla came up with the idea that since it was so hot they should have a barbeque for dinner. Meegan was in the kitchen, helping prepare the salad, whilst Aiden did the man thing and cooked the meat. He was flipping over the steaks, mulling over Brandy's case in his mind. If she really had been abused, there were hopefully some records to back up her claims: hospital files, police reports, probably disguised as 'accidents' rather than violently inflicted injuries.

The grey clouds had now swallowed the entire sky but the heat remained, and if anything had intensified. On his way home Aiden had dropped into work, only to find that neither Edmond nor Betty were there; just a brief note left to explain that the heat was too much and that they would see him tomorrow. However, Edmond had stated in the note that installing air conditioning was now on the top of his to do list! Aiden was grateful to be able to head home and get out of his suit. Standing outside in just a T-shirt and shorts he felt incredibly relaxed and settled in his new house. Avalon was a huge adjustment for the family but they seemed to be doing well.

'Baby, how are those steaks doing?' Isla called from the kitchen. Aiden skewered the largest steak with a knife, clear liquid oozed on to the burning coals below.

'Nearly done!' he shouted back.

'I want to see,' Meegan came running over on her podgy legs but Aiden held his hand up sternly.

'No, princess, it is too hot. Help Mommy with the salad.' She looked grumpy, and then her lip started to quiver and Aiden braced himself for the tantrum, but luckily Isla intervened.

'Want to help Mommy with the strawberries for dessert?'

'Strawberries!' Meegan cried gleefully, instantly forgetting her banishment from the barbeque area.

'Thanks for averting that storm,' Aiden laughed.

'No problem, don't think I can stop that one though,' she pointed out into the distance. Aiden looked up and sure enough, silver forks of lightning were dancing across the sky and didn't appear to be that far away.

'I'll just finish up here; we had better eat inside, just to be safe.'

The family were happily tucking into their steaks when rain started to lash at the windows.

'Here it comes,' Isla sighed.

'Here what comes?' her little daughter asked innocently.

'Just a storm, honey, nothing to worry about.'

Aiden found that he didn't have much of an appetite. Perhaps it was the heat, but he wagered that it had more to do with the uproar his mind was in.

'Babe, are you OK?' Isla asked, concerned over the amount of food left on his plate.

'I'm just not hungry.'

'Probably this heat'. He was glad that she wasn't going to interrogate him further.

'Although someone can still eat like a horse!' she rustled her daughter's hair, as the little girl proudly lifted up her empty plate.

'I like salad,' she told her parents.

'Good girl, fruit and vegetables will help you grow big and strong,' Aiden told her. Meegan raised her arms above her head, showing how big she already was.

'Wow, you are huge!' he laughed.

'Nobody is going to mess with our little girl,' Isla giggled. Aiden smiled but felt a pang of sadness wash over him. How would he feel if a man attacked Meegan? Small, innocent, beautiful Meegan. Surely any man who could raise his fists to a woman is a monster? If that is the case, then the heroic image Avalon had of Brandon White was all just a sham. How would the town feel towards Aiden if he shattered their dream of their golden boy?

'Penny for your thoughts?' Isla tapped his arm.

'Penny for your thoughts!' Meegan echoed.

'Nothing,' he told the two women in his life. 'Just work stuff.' Thunder rumbled from far away, a warning of what was the come. Meegan looked uneasy. She held her hands out to her mother, indicating that she wanted to be out of her high chair and safe in her arms.

'Why don't we all go sit in the living-room,' Isla offered, hoisting the toddler out. 'Aiden?'

'Yeah...sorry...I'm coming.'

'When you are with us, *be with us,*' she muttered to him angrily under her breath.

The rain intensified and as the thunder grew louder, flashes of lightning began to illuminate the sky. Meegan was nestled safely between her parents, cowering in fear at each rumble. Aiden had wanted to put the television on but Isla wouldn't allow him. So there they sat, waiting for the storm to pass. After a while even he had to admit that it was an immense storm. Once or twice he thought he heard trees splitting as they were struck by lightning. It was so dark it felt like the dead of night. Despite the noise, Meegan had managed to fall asleep, her hand on Aiden's chest.

'I'll take her up to bed,' he whispered.

'No, if she wakes up in bed and the storm is still raging she will be terrified. Leave her here till it passes,' his wife ordered.

They sat in near enough silence, for fear of waking Meegan. Aiden's thoughts drifted to Brandy, how she must have been terrified in her cell as the storm raged outside. At least he had Isla and Meegan, she had no one. He almost felt guilty that she was alone. No doubt the storm was bringing back memories of Brandon and that fateful night when he proposed. Aiden watched his wife. She was doing amazingly well and he should tell her that more often; there was no doubt that he could be a better husband. He leant over Meegan and squeezed Isla's hand. She repaid the gesture.

'Scared?' she teased.

'As long as I have you, what is there to be scared of?' Isla blushed.

'I don't mean to be distant, honey. Work is just a little heavy at the moment.'

'Well, it's OK, it will be over soon.' Over. The word lingered in Aiden's mind. It wasn't just the case that would be over, it would be Brandy's life. He shifted uncomfortably beneath his growing concerns.

'Aid, are you alright?'

'Yes, baby, just stiff beneath this weight,' he nodded towards a sleeping Meegan and laughed.

'I don't know how she does it, but that kid can sleep anywhere,' Isla said as she stroked her daughter's soft hair fondly.

Once the storm had finally passed Aiden tucked Meegan up in bed and went and grabbed a cool beer from the fridge. The tension in the air had lifted, leaving a calm atmosphere, full of hope and new beginnings. He was curious about the damage inflicted by the storm but by now it was too dark to go out exploring. He curled up on the sofa besides Isla. She was already on her second glass of wine and was getting sleepy.

'Baby, do you remember our wedding song?'

'You are my destiny, you are my one and only,' she softly sang the lyrics to the popular Lionel Richie song in response. He smiled and wrapped his arm around her.

'Remember how much my college buddies ribbed me about that?'

'But we did love a bit of Lionel. It was our guilty pleasure.' Her head was rested on his shoulder and Aiden breathed in the intoxicating aroma of her hair.

'The world always feels so peaceful after a storm,' she observed.

'I like it.'

'Me too. I'm going to start painting tomorrow now it won't be as hot. I got some moody blue, like you asked.'

'Great.'

'I'm thinking that will do for the bathroom.'

'Uh huh,' in the fading light outside stars began to pierce through the now departing clouds. Isla rubbed a hand along Aiden's inner thigh, but it was affectionate not suggestive. He could tell that tonight all they would be doing in bed was sleeping, and he was OK with that. It had been a stressful day and all he wanted to do was lay his head upon his pillow and drift away to somewhere free from the pain and strife of reality.

'You know what comes after a storm?' his wife mused in her sleepy, drunken haze.

'No, baby, what comes after a storm?'

'A rainbow. A beautiful, multi-colored rainbow that makes everything seem better.' Aiden could sense his own rainbow appearing. If Brandy could back up her claims about Brandon's violent nature, Aiden could save her from the gas chamber. And surely there is no greater calling than to save a life? With a new sense of purpose, he finished his beer and let sleep take hold as he lay with his wife sprawled across him. Outside, thunder rumbled in the distance, as the storm moved on, preparing to shake up another town.

Chapter Six

Superhuman?

Buck Fernlived and breathed Avalon. Nothing happened in the
town without him knowing about it and he liked it that way. He
felt that his dedication was what made him so good at his job.
He had held his position as sheriff for a good two decades.
People around town respected and trusted him. He upheld the
law and helped maintain the balance between right and wrong.
Buck enjoyed his job and felt that it gave his life purpose. There
were two things that he did not like; outsiders and those that
questioned him. Aiden Connelly was both of these things, which
meant that Buck disliked him intensely. When he saw the young
lawyer approaching the sheriff's office early Wednesday
morning his cursed under his breath. He knew from past
experience that people from the city always think that they know
best. They are quick to try and impress their fancy lifestyle and
way of thinking on to the people of Avalon. But there was a
system in town, and it worked. Buck had worked hard to instil
this system and he'd be damned if some hotshot kid was going
to try and undermine him. As Aiden pushed open the office
doors Buck tensed all over and prepared himself for what would
undoubtedly be an unpleasant encounter.

Aiden was relieved to find that since the storm the weather
was decidedly cooler. However, as he entered Avalon Sheriff's
Department, he felt that the air grew even colder as Buck Fern
gave him a frosty reception. Again, Aiden politely offered his
hand to the old man, who merely regarded it and grunted. Buck
was sat on a desk, rather than behind it, and when Aiden had
approached had appeared to be idly gazing out of the front
windows of the office.

'Must be a slow day,' Aiden mused to himself.

Buck made no attempt to hide his disdain for the young man. He didn't even raise himself from his perch when Aiden had entered, preferring to continue to gaze out of the window until his visitor was directly in front of him. Buck Fern was being downright rude; it was childish and uncalled for but it was all the old man knew. When he didn't like somebody, he either punched them square in the face, which, being sheriff, wasn't the best approach, or he did his best to completely ignore them. Aiden was being annoyingly persistent which meant that Buck had to reconsider his strategy. He would have loved nothing more than to wipe the smug look of his boyish face, but he knew that he needed to restrain himself, at least for the time being.

'We meet again, Sheriff.'

'So it would seem.'

'As you know, I'm currently in charge of the Brandy White case.'

'You did mention it.' Aiden felt his frustration growing. Dealing with Buck was like dealing with a petulant teenager, which was ridiculous considering he was a grown man and sheriff of a town no less! He was starting to think that coming to try and gather information from him was not a good idea.

'Then, you'll remember that I also mentioned that I'd be needing access to certain files relating to the case.'

Buck ran a wrinkled hand across his equally aged face and shot Aiden a dirty look.

'Protocol? He queried.

'Pretty much.'

'Pretty much?'

'I can't disclose any information to you I'm afraid. I trust that you will cooperate with my investigations?'

Buck raised himself up from the desk so that he was standing. Aiden assumed that this movement was meant to somehow intimidate him but it failed to have the desired effect.

'I need to have the files relating to the arrest of Brandy White, including the police report from the night of the murder.'

'Fine, I'll have those sorted out for you in due time.'

'Due time? I need those files quickly, so if you can make haste, Sheriff. The trial is in just over two weeks.'

'I'm aware of when the trial is. The whole town is. You will get your damn files when you get them.' Aiden didn't want to argue with the old man.

'I also need any other files regarding Brandon White.'

'Other files?' Buck seemed taken aback by this request.

'Yes, past indiscretions. Speeding fines, public disputes like bar fights, DUIs, anything like that.'

'What are you implying?'

Aiden was cautious not to give too much away. At least not yet.

'I need to have a clear legal history of both Brandy and Brandon. As I said, I can't tell you much, it is all part of my investigation.'

'Brandon never got in no trouble,' Buck hissed at him angrily.

'You are telling me that he was whiter than white?' The Sheriff remained silent. 'Yeah, I didn't think so.'

'This town loved Brandon.'

'So I keep hearing.'

'That devil woman murdered him in cold blood. What more do you need to know?'

'A lot more, actually. I'll come for the files tomorrow.'

'If I were you, I'd stop digging.'

'You don't scare me.'

'You going to the big game tonight, Mr. Connelly?' the change of topic caught Aiden off guard.

'Sorry?'

'The football game, over at the high school. Big event, the whole town comes out to give the boys some support. I expect you'll be taking your lovely wife and daughter along with you.'

'Are you threatening me?' Aiden asked, shocked.

'Heavens no,' Buck laughed, but there was a menacing glint in his eyes. 'I was just trying to make conversation. New kid in town, will do you good to go to the game, get in with the townsfolk. It is important to make friends somewhere as small as Avalon. You might try to remember that.'

'Thanks, I will,' Aiden was starting to become unnerved by Buck's behavior and didn't want to antagonize him further.

'I'll be going, then, I'll be back around the same time tomorrow.'

'Can't wait,' Buck called after him, sarcasm coating his words.

Aiden waved half-heartedly as he left, glad to be away, as he got back into his car and headed towards work.

'Good morning, Mr. Connelly,' Betty greeted him as he walked through the door. Now that the weather had cooled considerably she was back to her normal, immaculate self.

'Terrible storm last night.'

'Yes, it was, think we needed it though.'

'Well, I cannot bear the heat. Plays havoc with me! Oh, before you go in, you have a visitor in there waiting for you.'

'A visitor?' Aiden was intrigued.

'Yes, Father West arrived about ten minutes ago asking to see you. Edmond is out of the office for the morning and it didn't feel right leaving a man of God to wait out here on the sofas. Hope you don't mind. I've given him a cup of coffee. Would you believe that he takes two sugars?'

Aiden thanked Betty and headed into his office, puzzled at what this impromptu meeting with Father West could be about.

As Aiden entered the room Father West rose to his feet and extended his hand in greeting. They shook hands vigorously and exchanged pleasantries. Aiden was thankful for the gesture after his uncomfortable encounter with Buck Fern. Even dressed down in jeans and a blue shirt, Father West's dog collar still gave him away. Aiden noted again how devastatingly handsome he was. He couldn't help but wonder what had made him choose this particular path in life, he was certain that priests could not enjoy the company of a woman until they entered into marriage, and looking like he did, Father West would certainly find temptation around every corner. Aiden toyed with the idea that perhaps, if the two men managed to strike up a friendship, he may one day be able to ask him what drew him to devote his life to God. He was genuinely curious.

'So, to what do I owe this pleasure?' Aiden asked as he settled himself behind his desk.

'How are you settling into town?'

'Fine,' Aiden replied, bemused. Surely, Father West had not troubled himself to come into his offices just to enquire about his well-being?

'I was glad that you came to church on Sunday.'

'We never normally go. But, a new start and everything, can't hurt to have God on your side.'

Father West smiled. 'It will be good for you and your family to meet people from around town. Your wife must be feeling quite isolated.'

A shiver crept up Aiden's spine as he feared that he had grossly misjudged Father West. The next thing he knew, he would be offering to stop by his house and keep Isla company during the day and one thing would lead to another...

Aiden cursed himself for being so childish.

'Perhaps she may like to join the gardening club that a few of the local ladies set up?'

'Yes, might be good. We need to start looking into nurseries for our daughter.'

'I could recommend a few.'

'That would be great.'

Aiden watched Father West drain his coffee cup and sensed that the priest wanted to say something more.

'You enjoy working here?'

'Sure do,' Aiden was growing tired of the biennial questions regarding his life. 'Edmond is a great man, I'm enjoying working with him immensely.'

'Didn't you say that you were handling the Brandy White case?' Bingo. Father West was here to dig.

'Yeah, I am. It is an interesting one. Have you been over to Eastham to see her yet?'

'No, but I will as soon as I can.'

'She would really appreciate that.'

'Yes.'

'I imagine she is in a very dark place.' Father West merely nodded. 'You knew her well, didn't you, Father?'

84

'She attended church regularly when she was younger, yes,' Aiden couldn't help but notice that Father West was blushing profusely.

'Wasn't it you that had her mother sectioned?' The dynamic of the conversation had changed, placing Father West in the hot seat.

'Yes, many years ago. Janice Cotton. Poor woman had truly lost her way, sad that she never returned. You can only hope that wherever she is, she is doing better than she was.'

'Indeed.' Aiden was still unsure as to why Father West had come to see him. He felt uneasy quizzing a priest but continued none the less.

'And weren't you the priest who married Brandy and Brandon?'

'Yes, I was,' Father West looked sad. Or did he look guilty? Aiden couldn't tell.

'How well did you know Brandon?'

'Not very well.'

'It seems like he was very popular around town.'

'Yes, he was.'

The two men sat in silence for a moment. Father West was struggling with a number of things, least of all his conscience. Aiden Connelly had barely been in town five minutes; it would be foolish to assume that he could trust him. Yet Patrick West had always prided himself on being an accurate judge of character. His instincts had almost always been right, sometimes to the point where he found himself resenting the profession he was in. Too many people came and sat before him to profess their love and devotion to God, whilst hiding a multitude of sins.

'Brandy says that Brandon hit her,' Aiden felt the words shoot out of his mouth before he had chance to think. Father West's eyebrows rose in surprise, but his face remained deadpan, leading Aiden to believe what he had suspected; that Father West already knew.

'She told you that?'

'Yes, and she has marks all up her arms. I've no doubt that there are more. I'm hoping to go and see her again tomorrow.'

85

Silence once again settled amongst them. Both men, in their minds, said a thousand words, but neither knew how to vocalize their thoughts to the other. Finally, Father West spoke.

'Brandy led a very troubled life…'

'Yeah, I know all about the beauty pageant scandal and her mother; what I'm talking about is her marriage.'

'Even after her vows,' Father West concluded.

'So you knew about the abuse?' The priest suddenly looked his age, worn down by the burden of carrying other people's troubles for so long.

'She came to me, often very distraught, saying she had fallen over, or walked into a wall. But I knew.'

'Why didn't you do anything?'

'What could I do? I'm her priest. She came to me in confidence, and never directly blamed Brandon.'

'Everyone around here sees him as some kind of saint,' Aiden felt anger boiling up in his blood. 'How bad was it?'

'I don't know.' Father West was lying, he sensed it. Aiden was growing tired of playing games with him.

'Father, why did you come here?' There it was, blunt and to the point. He expected Father West to be taken aback by the question, instead he nodded thoughtfully.

'I'm wondering that too,' he drummed his fingers against his coffee cup as his mind worked furiously to seek an answer.

'You are new in town and handling a very sensitive case. I guess, what I'm trying to say is…listen to Brandy. Let her tell her story. People around here are so quick to judge, but there is more to this than meets the eye.'

'You know more than you are saying,' Aiden accused.

'That is all I can tell you for now. Just be careful. Brandon was loved by this town, and some people would do anything to see Brandy go down.'

'Like Sheriff Fern?'

'He can be dangerous.' Aiden was beginning to feel uneasy. Was Father West warning him? Had Buck Fern sent him? He didn't know what to think.

'Can I trust you?' the question caught Aiden off guard. Here he was, wondering if the priest was on his side, whilst all along Father West had been thinking the same thing of him.

'As long as I can trust you.'

'Good, then we will talk again. First, you need to see Brandy. Tell her to tell you everything. Tell her you have spoken with me.' They shook hands, only this time with more sincerity.

'Take care, Mr. Connelly. May God be with you.'

Aiden felt shell-shocked after speaking with Father West. In the tranquility of the empty office his mind was a tangled maze of questions, but one thing he knew was that Brandy held a majority of the answers. He was debating going over to Eastham that very afternoon when Edmond came through the door, a beaming smile across his face, followed by two men in blue overalls.

'Well, Aiden my boy, I've gone and done it!' He clapped his hands together in glee.

'Done what?'

'Today, a momentous occasion,' he began as Betty came in to see what all the commotion was.

'I am bringing this office into the 21st century. We are having air conditioning installed!'

'Oh how simply marvellous!' Betty cried out in glee.

'In your own time boys,' he said to the workmen, enjoying his moment of empowerment.

'Coffees?' Betty asked excitedly.

'Thanks, hon,' the workmen accepted her offer gratefully. Edmond and Aiden both decided to indulge in a caffeine fix also.

'This heatwave made me realize it was high time we modernized the office,' Edmond was explaining. 'I thought it would be a nice surprise for you all!'

'Very thoughtful of you, Edmond.'

'Thanks, my lad. Now we can work in a cool, calm environment. I think it is a fantastic investment. It was Betty really that swayed me. The old girl told me she was worried she was suffering from heat exhaustion!'

'Really?'

'Said she was feeling faint, having shortness of breath. Sounds like the change to me, but you can't say that to a lady. My wife taught me that the hard way!' He chuckled to himself.

'Well then, let's get down to it. The law doesn't represent itself, you know!' Edmond sneakily made his coffee Irish; he was tempted to extend this offer to Aiden, but the lad seemed distant, so he thought better of it.

Aiden decided against visiting Brandy that afternoon. He decided that he first wanted to speak with Clyde White again, and the football game that evening would give him the perfect opportunity.

It was the night of the big game and the air buzzed with electric tension. Aiden, like many other residents of Avalon, had driven to the high school, parked up and was now walking towards the football field. For such a small town there was certainly an impressive turnout. The game didn't start until seven; Aiden had arrived at a quarter past six, on Edmond's advice, and had still struggled to find a parking space. He could already hear a steady chorus of chanting coming from up ahead. It was a modest football field, flanked on two sides by tiered seating. The floodlights were already on as dusk was disappearing fast, being replaced by the dark void of night.

Meegan was finding it all quite wonderful. Seated high up on her father's shoulders she was merrily waving a small flag an avid fan had kindly given her when they had arrived. There was a slight chill in the air so the family had layered up in sweaters, knowing that when standing around at night, you can get very cold, very quickly.

Aiden had anticipated that a majority of the crowd would be high school students, but he couldn't have been more wrong. The game attracted fans young and old alike, in fact, the students appeared to be outnumbered by the more senior residents which he found amusing. Everyone was in good spirits, exchanging kind hellos and the more excitable already whooping and cheering. Aiden had missed all this, the sense of community. Isla, however, didn't appear to be having a good time.

'It is all very loud,' she whispered to Aiden as they sat down in the bleachers. He could tell from her tone that she was annoyed. She hadn't wanted to come. Isla was never one for sports, that, as she put it; 'You had to drink beer to enjoy.' Aiden had always loved football; he had even played in high school. Admittedly he wasn't very good, but he had loved it all the same.

'Just try and relax, honey, have a good time,' he said to his wife. He now had Meegan on his lap but she was throwing herself around everywhere.

'Oi,' he said to her sternly. 'Stop wriggling like a worm!'

'But I want to see the fussble.'

'We will see the football in a minute. The players will only come out if you sit down like a good little girl.' Meegan huffed but did as her father said.

'Didn't you go to many games when you were at school?' he asked Isla.

'Nope. We were a basketball school.'

'Oh, right. I guess you are quite tall!'

'Fool! I didn't play!' she nudged him playfully.

'Ladies and Gentlemen!' A voice beamed from the overhead speakers. Meegan cowered in terror.

'For your entertainment, your Avalon Angels Cheering Squad!' The crowd erupted in cheers, some more zealous people even rose to their feet and wolf-whistled.

A dozen teenage girls, dressed in skimpy red and white dresses, came out on to the field and took up formation before the home team.

'Give me an A!' shouted a perky blonde at the front.

'A!' the crowd echoed. Aiden chanted along and watched as the cheerleaders cartwheeled and pivoted around the field, building up support for their team and remembered all too fondly how much he loved cheerleaders.

In high school, being on the football team meant two things: you got to cut classes and you got laid. In his experience, all the stereotypes regarding cheerleaders had been wonderfully true, and watching this gaggle of gorgeous girls dancing before him he couldn't help but hope that Isla had once been a cheerleader and that she had kept her uniform...

After the cheerleading routine the voice returned from the heavens, this time to announce the arrival of the Avalon Angels football team. This time the crowd went wild; everyone was on their feet, Aiden and Isla included. He was glad to see that she was finally entering into the spirit of things.

The strapping lads of the football team were full of youth and energy. Aiden envied them. If only the feelings of euphoria you experience as a teenager could be crystallized and you could keep it with you forever. But then he remembered the more awkward memories high school can bring: from your first kiss to an outbreak of acne. He was glad to be beyond the learning stage of life, although it scared him to think that in the not too distant future Meegan would be experiencing all the things that he did.

'Aid, I'm having trouble following the game,' Isla confided ten minutes in. Aiden did his best to relay to her the rules regarding American football but it was difficult to be heard over the whoops and chanting of the crowd. He concluded that he probably should have explained the basics to her before they had left the house.

As the third quarter got under way Aiden turned his attention away from the game and started seeking out familiar faces in the crowd; in particular he was looking for Clyde White. From where he was sitting there was no sign of him; he did, however, spot Edmond and his family who waved enthusiastically. Thankfully he couldn't see Buck Fern.

'Daddy, I'm tired,' Meegan moaned, flopping her head dramatically against her father's chest.

'I know baby, not long now.' The crowd were now more subdued as the Avalon Angels were trailing behind. The cheerleaders did their best to rally support but as the closing minutes ticked by, the home team had to admit defeat. Disheartened, the people of Avalon began returning to their cars. Heads lbent down in shame, the football players cleared the field, although Aiden noticed them quickly perk up as the cheerleaders came skipping over to lick their wounds and massage their egos.

Meegan was now fast asleep as they made their way with the crowd towards the parking lot.

'Is your daughter ever awake?' a friendly voice called.

'Oh, Father West,' Isla grinned girlishly. Aiden nodded in greeting.

'Did you enjoy the game? Shame we didn't win.'

'It was good. The team are pretty popular.'

'They sure are. A decent team this year, some impressive players coming along.'

'The team got a lot of history?' Father West eyed Aiden nervously at this question.

'Most men in Avalon played for the Angels at some point, so everyone has a personal connection and knows somebody playing in it now, be it a son, nephew or neighbor.'

'Right, right.'

'Did you notice the black armbands?'

'Yeah, for Brandon?'

'Yeah.' The two men exchanged knowing glances. Aiden was going to say more when Father West was dragged into conversation with an elderly man, who was being quite vocal in his complaint about the upkeep of his late wife's grave stone. Aiden felt sorry for Father West, he must feel that he is at work 24/7. Although he would probably feed him some line like 'Doing the Lord's work is no chore.' Aiden knew that his lack of patience would prevent him from doing any such job. He got annoyed even at dinner parties when, as soon as people get wind that you are a lawyer, start asking for legal advice.

Aiden had just settled Meegan into her car seat when Edmond cornered him.

'Well, hello there, my boy! I hope you enjoyed your first game!' Aiden almost reeled back from the smell of liquor on his colleagues' breath.

'Having a good night, Edmond?'

'Splendid, splendid. Shame we lost, but you can't win them all! My dear!' he exclaimed as he saw Isla, before promptly wrapping his arms around her. Her eyes looked pleadingly at Aiden as she was stuck fast in Edmond's embrace.

'Such a great game,' he said as he finally let her go. 'I told Betty she should come, but she said it isn't her thing. Yet I invite her, every game. The old girl needs to get out more!'

'I thought Clyde White would be here but I haven't seen him.' Aidan noted.

'Clyde? Yes, he is normally always here. The team means a lot to him. He's probably here somewhere.' Aiden scanned the assortment of people bustling around him into various vehicles but could see no sign of the Avalon Pine owner.

'Ed, Ed!' a female voice was calling. 'Oh there you are!' Carol Copes came staggering over, equally as drunk as Edmond was.

'Oh, Aiden, hello!' This time it was his turn for the over-familiar embrace. Squashed up against Carol's ample bosom he could see his wife giggling.

'Hello, Carol, good to see you again,' he said timidly once she had let him go and he had refilled his lungs.

'Well, we best be off,' Edmond bowed and linked arms with his wife and the pair tilted left, then right before aligning themselves and wandering off.

'Quite a pair, aren't they?' Isla laughed.

'Sure are.'

'Meegan told me that she wants to be a cheerleader.'

'Oh no,' Aiden said as he got into the car. 'I know what cheerleaders are like and my daughter will be a lady!' Isla giggled at this.

'Why did you want to see Clyde White?' she asked as they were driving along.

'No reason,' Aiden lied. 'Just work stuff.' Isla rolled her eyes.

'Don't you ever clock off?' she moaned.

'Yes, of course. I just wanted to ask him something, that's all.'

'Well, I'm sure it can wait.'

'Yes, I guess it will have to.'

Aiden's car rolled along the darkened streets until they were back home. That night his sleep was troubled, his dreams haunted by demonic football players. He awoke in a sweat, gasping for breath. Isla remained curled up beside him, peaceful in her slumber. Alone, he turned his mind to Clyde White. He was certain that he had not been present at the game. If this was the case, Aiden could only come to one of two conclusions to explain his absence; possibly Clyde was sick, which he doubted as he had only seen him not long before, and he was fit and well. Which left Aiden to believe that Clyde had not attended the game because he was avoiding him. Which meant that he had something to hide.

Chapter Seven

Shattered Glass

It was an unseasonably cold morning when Aiden drove out to Eastham. The sun was refusing to show her face and dark grey clouds dominated the sky. The roads were empty as usual as he made his way towards the prison which was Brandy's cage.

Aiden took up his usual position before the Perspex glass wall, carefully setting up his Dictaphone and arranging his notes before Prisoner 929's arrival. The walls were as dull as the sky outside, as if all colors had been drained away from the world. Eastham felt even more oppressive than usual. One of the guards announced Brandy's arrival but he need not have bothered, the moment she entered the room it was as if the entire universe shifted. She appeared to be glowing, from her luminous hair to the harsh orange of her regulation clothing. It felt as if Brandy was the sun in a dark, never-ending universe and you could not help but be drawn to her. Her cheeks were flushed and she seemed happy, and Aiden felt his heart soar. He berated himself for it, but couldn't help feeling a sense of delight at seeing that Brandy was happy. Even the guards seemed in a more favourable mood. Brandy was blissfully unaware of the power she held over them all as she delicately sat down and gazed at Aiden, awaiting his direction for how the meeting was to proceed.

'So, Brandy, how are you feeling today?' he knew he was making small talk and wasting valuable time but he couldn't help it.

'Today, Mr. Connelly, I am feeling mighty fine. I feel as if that storm took all my problems away with it.'

'That is good to hear.' He shuffled his papers nervously, apprehensive about carrying on. Brandy seemed to be in a good place, and he knew that what he needed to ask her, what he needed her to recall, would no doubt return her to the darkest place she had ever been, and guilt overwhelmed him.

'I went to the game last night.' He was stalling.

'Oh, the Angels? Oh wow, I bet you had a real good time! Everyone loves the Angels!'

'Did you used to go watch them?'

'Sometimes, not all that much. I never was around enough to get caught up in that whole school spirit thing.'

Aiden took a deep breath; he needed to get answers, even if that meant stealing the sparkle from her eyes.

'Brandy,' he spoke softly, 'I need you to tell me, in detail, about your marriage to Brandon.'

As Aiden had feared, at the mention of Brandon the glow within Brandy immediately vanished and the room plunged into a depressive state of darkness. Her eyes became dark and her skin grey.

'Very well, Mr. Connelly,' her voice was calm and steady. 'But I must warn you, it isn't a pretty tale to tell.' And with her warning out of the way, she recalled her time as Mrs. Brandon White.

'As I told you, Brandon liked a drink. He always had. His drinking got him in trouble all over town, drink driving and the like. But old Buck Fern always turned the other cheek, his status as a football hero made him almost untouchable. He was used to always getting his own way, when people went against him, he would lash out. Not at them, just me. At first it was just words, which I could handle. If he'd had a bad day at work he'd come in, shouting, swearing. Then the anger was directed at me; he'd call me stupid, lazy, that sort of thing. After that, he grew violent, throwing things around, smashing glasses. At this point I wasn't too bothered. I could see that he had a temper and when he was in one of his foul moods I'd just stay away from him. Normally, he was still the sweetest man in the world so I could

95

easily forgive him for a few cruel words. But then, about eight months after we had gotten married, he turned on me.'

Aiden wished he could pass his hand through the glass and hold hers but he couldn't; she had to push through the pain of her memories alone.

'I can still remember that night. I wish I'd had the strength then to pack my bags and leave but I had nowhere to go. He was my everything. He knew that, I think that was how he knew he could get away with treating me how he did. He had been out with his friends and he was very drunk. He came in demanding that I cook him dinner, so I told him that he'd had dinner before he went out. Well, that was enough to send him crazy. His eyes got all screwed up in rage, he called me a lying whore and a bitch, then he punched me square in the face. The force threw me on to my back and I just lay there in shock. He yelled at me to get up but I was afraid. When I wouldn't get up he kicked me in my sides. The pain was unbearable, I felt like all my insides were being crushed. After a bit he got bored and wandered off into the bedroom where he collapsed on the bed.'

'The next day, I looked so awful that I was too ashamed to leave and seek help, I didn't want anyone seeing me like that. I had two black eyes, a cut lip and my whole body was beaten black and blue. I ran myself a bath and just lay in it, crying for hours. When Brandon sobered up he couldn't apologize enough. He brought me flowers, told me how much he loved me, that he would never touch me again.'

She pressed her palms against her eyes, holding back tears. 'He lied.'

'So, that was the first time he was violent towards you?' Aiden asked gently. Brandy nodded in response.

'But soon,' she breathed in deeply, trying to stop her emotions overwhelming her, 'it became a regular thing. Most weekends he would knock me about so that I stopped leaving the house at all, for fear of people seeing me. Each time it was the same, he would attack me in rage, then later tell me how sorry he was and that he would get help. I wanted to go to someone, but foolishly I believed that he could change. How could I have been so stupid?'

'Did you tell anyone?'

'Yes, in the end I felt that he'd left me with no choice. It was my 20th birthday and he was supposed to finish work early and take me for dinner and a movie. I was all dressed up in the nicest dress I had and so excited about finally getting out of the damn house. I told myself that this was beginning of something good with Brandon, that we were beginning to put all our problems behind us. Well, six o'clock came and went and he didn't come home.

It was eleven when he came rolling in through the door. He was blind drunk as he had been out with boys. I was fuming. I asked where he'd been and he flipped. I'd never seen him so mad before, he was like a monster. We had a beautiful glass vase on the table; it had been a wedding gift, full of his last batch of forgiveness flowers. He grabbed the vase and smashed it against the wall. I was devastated, so I fell to my knees and began trying to pick up the shards of glass. I loved that vase, so much,' Brandy was crying now, tears forming a river down her soft cheeks.

'He yelled at me, saying I cared more for the vase then him. Then he...he...' she wiped her eyes with the sleeve of her jumpsuit. 'He knelt down and picked up a large shard of glass and ran it down my arm,' she pulled up her sleeve to reveal a frighteningly large scar. 'He did it all down my legs too. When he was satisfied that he had punished me enough he went and got into the shower. I had no choice but to call 911, I was going to bleed to death.'

'So the police came round?'

'Sheriff Fern himself came out. When he asked what had happened Brandon was cool as a cucumber, saying that the vase had fallen on to me by accident. I screamed that he was lying, that he had done this. Brandon, still so terribly calm, said that I was just trying to get back at him for forgetting my birthday. Buck Fern sided with Brandon, saying that women can get far too emotional and that I should be less clumsy. They took me to the hospital and dressed my wounds and no one said anymore about it. I thought that Brandon would be mad, but for a while he calmed down. I expect it had all been a bit too close a call for him and he was worried about being found out.'

Aiden was writing away in his notebook.

'What date is your birthday?'

'March 18th.' He scribbled the date down. 'You thinking of sending me a card?' she smiled weakly, her eyes red from crying.

'Maybe,' Aiden replied, aware that she would probably not live to see her next birthday. 'I'm actually interested as there would be a police report from when you called for the police and I'd like to see it.'

'Oh, OK.'

'So how was Brandon after that had happened?'

'Like I said, for a while he seemed to calm down. Then maybe a month or so later the drunken beatings returned. He had taken to smoking now too so he was getting creative with his cruelty, sometimes burning me. I was getting pretty scarred up by this time. I couldn't wear t-shirts or pretty dresses anymore as my arms and legs were such a mess. If people suspected anything no one dared say a word against Brandon. Even in searing heat I'd be wearing jeans and a sweater. But then, around Christmas time, I found out I was pregnant. I was overjoyed, I thought that a baby would help calm Brandon down, and that in carrying our baby he would ease off on me. And he did. For the first few months he was wonderful, he even painted the spare bedroom blue as he was convinced we were going to have a little boy. But then…he started drinking again…as I got bigger he would call me fat, telling me that he didn't find me attractive anymore. He made me cover up my bump in baggy clothes as he didn't want no one knowing I was pregnant. He said he was tired of the town always being all over his business. He started beating me again, but he was always careful to just do my legs and arms, where no one could see.'

Brandy was subconsciously rubbing her arms as she recalled her husband's cruelty.

'Then, he had to go away one weekend, it was around Easter. I think it was something to with work. I saw my chance to finally go to church; I hadn't been in so long. And now that I was expecting a child, I knew I needed to find peace with God again, for the sake of my unborn baby. I walked all the way into town; my feet were near bleeding by the time I got there. I just sat in a pew, shattered, when Father West came over. He was worried as he hadn't seen me in a long time. I was so hot, it was a warm day, I was sweating like a dog from all the walking, and without thinking I rolled up my sleeves. I heard him gasp when he saw my arms and my heart sunk.'

'Did you tell Father West what had been going on?'

'I had no choice. You can't lie to a priest. When he saw that I was pregnant too, he was outraged. He begged me to leave him, he said he would find somewhere safe for me to go but I wouldn't have it. I knew how hard it was to grow up without a father and I didn't want to do that to my child. I was a fool; if I'd run away when I had the chance things would have been so different...' her voice trailed off, wracked with emotion.

'What did Father West do?' Aiden felt terrible at pushing her to continue but knew that their time would soon be up.

'He said he would talk to Brandon. And he did. He came round one day; it was another gorgeous, sunny day. They sat and talked, I was hanging laundry out to dry in the garden so I've no idea what was said. With Father West, Brandon was all smiles, the perfect gentleman. Then, as he waved goodbye to Father, he closed the door and turned to me, his smile was gone and his eyes were black with hate. He was beyond furious that I had gone to Father West. He said that he was going to teach me a lesson. He went out back and when he came back,' Brandy shook her head through the tears, still in disbelief at just how cruel her husband had been, 'when he came back he had a shovel.'

Aiden wasn't sure if he could bear to hear anymore. Brandy became engulfed by her tears, unable to continue. He could only imagine what had occurred after the priest had left.

After a while, the tears subsided.

'They took me to hospital, but I lost the baby,' she whispered. 'Brandon said I'd fallen down the stairs. He said that if I told anyone about him again he'd kill me, and I knew that he would. I lived in fear of him. You know the worst part?'

'What was the worst part?'

'That no one would believe that he could have done these things. He said that I fell down the stairs. Thing is, we don't have no stairs. But no one questioned him, and I was too scared to say anything.'

'Did you plan to kill him?'

'No, but he was about to kill me. I had no choice.'

Their time was up and an emotionally drained Brandy was led away, leaving Aiden with a lot to think about.

As Aiden had expected, Buck Fern was nowhere to be seen when he arrived at the sheriff's offices to collect the files he had requested. A polite young girl who was working there kindly informed him that he was off doing his daily rounds of Avalon. Aiden was relieved. His encounters with the old sheriff were becoming increasingly strained and he just wasn't in the mood for another awkward conversation. He just wanted to get the files and go. He waited patiently whilst the girl wandered into a back room to get his documents for him. As the minutes passed by he felt anger welling up inside him, as he thought that the stubborn old sheriff had failed to sort out the files for him in a deliberate attempt to withhold evidence. Luckily, just as his patience was about to wear out, the girl returned, laden down with numerous cardboard folders.

'Here you are, Mr. Connelly. I'm afraid that these aren't the originals; we can only let photocopies out of the building you see. So these are yours to keep.'

Taking the files, Aiden thanked her and left, feeling slightly annoyed that he wasn't being given access to the original files, feeling sure that this was just a ploy to keep something vital hidden from him.

Sat at his desk in his now cool office, Aiden began going over the police reports. Edmond was in court all day so he had the place to himself. Betty bustled in and out with coffee a few times, but apart from that he was undisturbed.

There were no surprises amongst the reports. Brandon had, as Aiden had suspected, had a few run-ins with the law. Nothing too serious, a few DUIs, two counts of being drunk and disorderly in a public place. It was always the same outcome; Brandon was given a verbal warning and a smack on the wrists. Each time the arresting officer was Buck Fern. This was probably just a coincidence, since it was a small town with an equally small police department, but Aiden wasn't convinced.

He flicked through the files until he found what he was looking for. March 18th. He opened the folder and began to read.

At 11:52pm, a 911 call from a woman at a local residence saying she had been attacked. Possible domestic dispute. Sheriff Fern and Officers Bark and Simmons were dispatched to investigate.

Aiden read on…

Sheriff Fern arrived at the scene at 00:03am. Shortly followed by Officers Bark and Simmons. A young woman was severely wounded by cut glass from a fallen vase. No sign of foul play. Woman sent to St. Mary's Hospital for further treatment. Outcome; severe accidental damage. No further investigation required.

The report was signed off by Buck Fern, but what intrigued Aiden was how the Sheriff had arrived on the scene before his deputies. Had he quickly constructed a cover-up story with Brandon to protect him? It just didn't add up. After March 18th there were no further incidents, at least none that had been documented. Aiden thought about the second time that Brandy said she had ended up in hospital, when she had lost her baby, but there was no record of any police involvement that time.

Aiden wasn't sure what to think, but he knew one thing, that Brandy was telling the truth. In his line of work, he rarely listened to his gut instinct, but this time it was screaming at him. It was clear that Brandon had beaten her; what he was unsure of was why anyone would want to cover it up. He read through the file again, St. Mary's Hospital treated Brandy after the attack on her birthday. Perhaps the files that they held would have more answers; also, if they were the nearest hospital, it was logical to think that they had treated Brandy when she 'fell down the stairs'.

'Betty?' he peered round his office door and could see the elderly lady typing away at her computer.

'Oh, Mr. Connelly,' she stopped immediately on hearing his voice. 'Another coffee? I'll get it for you right away!'

'No, no coffee, thanks. I actually need directions as I'll be out of the office this afternoon.'

'Directions. Certainly. To where?'

'St. Mary's Hospital.' Betty regarded him with a worried expression.

'Is everything all right, Mr. Connelly?'

'Yes, yes, everything is fine. I just need to go there, following a lead. It is all regarding the case.'

'Oh right, yes, well St. Mary's is a good few miles away. It will take you at least an hour to get there.'

Aiden checked his watch. It was already 2pm which didn't leave him much time but he knew that he needed to go there.

'It is always a bother for folks round here when they have to go to the hospital,' she continued. 'A couple of years ago, my left foot was playing up and I was back and forth for appointments. Ridiculous. Our doctor round here is too quick to send people for referrals. Good hospital though. Very modern,' she was talking as the directions were printing out of the printer located by her feet. Once it had finished, she whipped out the sheet and handed Aiden the neatly typed directions.

'I'm afraid we don't have a map, but if you have any trouble at all, just call. Edmond often has to head over to St. Mary's, usually with clients injured at work or whatever who want to file a complaint from their hospital bed! I tell you now, if I were in the hospital a lawsuit would be the last thing on my mind! But you know how people are...'

'Yes, well thank you, Betty.'

'Watch how you go, Mr. Connelly.'

Betty watched the handsome young lawyer leave, knowing that if she were twenty years younger she would be offering to do a whole lot more than print directions for him, whether he was married or not. She sighed wistfully, her mind drifting away to indulge in memories of her youth. As Aiden drove away, she decided that her afternoon would be much better spent at home, rather than lingering in an empty office with only her memories for company. She promptly switched off her computer, slung her handbag over her shoulder and locked up Cope and May Attorneys at Law for the day. Any urgent legal matters the people of Avalon had would have to wait until the following day.

It was 3:15pm when Aiden pulled into the parking lot of St. Mary's Hospital. Having been driving for just over an hour he felt groggy and tired. Luckily, the cool, crisp air that greeted him as he exited his car quickly revived him from his daze. As Betty had told him, St. Mary's was an impressive, modern hospital. However, now that he was here, he was unsure where to go. He decided that Reception would be his best bet.

'Yes?' the receptionist, a fat man with an acne-ridden face and glasses asked, clearly not interested in Aiden's response.

'I was wondering if you could help me?' he began.

'Patient name?' the man said in a deadpan voice, as if it was the hundredth time today he had been approached with the same query.

'No, I'm not looking for a patient. I'm looking for the...archive section...where files for past patients are kept.'

The man eyed him with disdain.

'I'm a lawyer,' Aiden explained, hoping to hurry the guy up a bit. The receptionist rolled his eyes in a bored manner and began typing into his computer.

'Down the corridor, left, three doors down on the right.'

'Right, OK, thanks,' Aiden headed off along the hospital corridors, following the directions until he came to a door labeled Patient Enquiries. He reasoned that this must be the place and knocked briskly on the door.

A middle-aged woman with a blonde perm answered. 'Can I help you?'

'Yes, I hope so, I need to have access to some files on someone who was a patient here.'

'That sort of information is classified,' she said as she eased the door behind her closed, as if fearing that Aiden was some crazy man who would rush her at any moment in an attempt to get to the files she presided over.

'I'm the lawyer of the patient in question.'

'I see, so you have made an appointment to view the files and have written consent from your client?'

'Well...no,' Aiden was starting to feel very foolish. He was all too aware of protocol when it came to the disclosure of sensitive information. He had been careless and too impetuous in heading out here without properly thinking it through. He was better than this; it wasn't like him to behave in such an unprofessional manner. However, now that he had come all this way he wasn't prepared to leave empty-handed. He didn't know if he would have another chance to come all the way out to St. Mary's again before the trial, which was now just over a week away. He needed to see Brandy's files; he had no time to waste.

'The thing is...' as he began the woman sighed, clearly annoyed that he was continuing to waste her time. 'This is a highly sensitive, high profile case. I couldn't risk you knowing about my arrival in case the media got wind of it.'

'I can assure you that we deal with all our patients with the highest level of confidentiality!' she said indignantly.

'I have no doubt,' Aiden was uncomfortable conducting their conversation in the hospital corridor with people frequently bustling past them. 'But it was a risk I couldn't take. A woman's life is at stake. I really have no time, please. I know I'm asking a lot of you,' he flashed her his most dashing smile and it seemed to work as her shoulders sunk in defeat.

'Luckily for you, Mr....'

'Connelly,'

'Luckily for you, Mr. Connelly, I'm in a good mood today. I can give you twenty minutes with the files you want, no more.' He thanked her as she opened the door and led him into a small room which was a hallway to another room, which was currently locked. This door was flanked by two desks, at one the woman presumably sat; she instructed Aiden to make himself comfortable at the other as she went to get his requested files. When he said Brandy's name he watched for any flicker of recognition at the name but she didn't show any signs of being aware of the scandal. But then this wasn't Avalon. Brandy's case was probably small news, if newsworthy at all.

It wasn't long before Aiden was gazing down at the patient files for Brandy White nee Cotton. Her patient history wasn't that extensive. The incident with the glass vase had been her first admission. She had been treated for severe cuts and abrasions, needing numerous stitches and a blood transfusion. She was then kept in under observation for two nights. As he scanned the notes he saw that at one point there had been a request by the on call doctor for a psychiatric consult to come and see Brandy. They must have thought that she had done it to herself. However, she was discharged before she was seen. It was noted that her body was covered in multiple bruises which weren't related to the smashed vase accident, but the doctor seemed to reach the wrong conclusion, that Brandy was self-harming. There was no connection made to Brandon at all.

The second time Brandy had been admitted was when she had lost her baby. The report made for more interesting reading:

Female, 22, came in after falling at home. Took a huge blow to the stomach. Was measuring at 24 weeks pregnant. Emergency ultrasound shows that baby did not survive the blow. Female also has numerous lacerations and bruising on body consistent with self, or inflicted abuse.

Note – to contact Avalon police department in order to pursue further enquiry after discharge.

Aiden reread the last statement, shock and surprise surging through his body. So, the hospital made the connection and contacted Buck Fern. And what did he do about it? According to the police files, he did nothing. But here was proof that he was aware of the situation of the young White couple. The old sheriff was undoubtedly withholding information from Aiden.

'May I please take a copy of this?'

'Yes, if you are quick, the copier is just there.' The woman pointed to a bulky machine in the far corner. Aiden hurriedly made a copy of both documents.

'Thank you so much,' he told her as he gathered his things to leave. 'You may well have just saved somebody's life.'

When Aiden arrived home, drained and exhausted, his tea lay waiting on the table and a sleeping Isla and Meegan were laid out on the couch. It was fairly late; it was seven when he got in, he had got stuck in traffic, so he just sat down to eat his dinner alone.

He must have made too much noise as a grumpy looking Isla soon came in to join him, rubbing her eyes.

'I had tea ready at half five as you had said you'd be finishing early today. I called the office but there was no one there.'

'Sorry, babe,' Aiden mumbled between mouthfuls.

'Where were you?'

'At the hospital.'

'The hospital?' He got up and fetched himself a beer and took a refreshing swig from the bottle before answering his wife.

'Don't worry, I'm OK, it was to do with the case.'

'The case, oh, of course,' she said bitterly.

'Don't be like that.'

'You could have let me know you'd be home late.'

'I got stuck in traffic.' Isla was pouting in annoyance. He reached out across the table and grabbed her hand. 'I'm sorry I should have called. But thanks so much for dinner honey, it is just what I needed.'

'Well, thank God dinner is on the table!' Isla yelled, pulling away from his hand and rising to her feet. 'I'm just being a good little wifey and doing my bit for my big, working husband!'

'Isla, calm down, you'll wake Meegan.'

'Well, you don't want that, because then you'll have to bother yourself with putting her to bed, better she stay sleeping!

Makes it easier for you, maybe I should have just stayed asleep too!'

'You're being ridiculous,' he snapped angrily. Fatigue was setting in and he hadn't the energy to argue with her but she was testing his patience.

'No, you are the ridiculous one, Aid. Coming home at all hours and thinking it is fine!'

'All hours, Isla, it is seven! I used to come home much later than this in Chicago!'

'But this isn't Chicago, is it? You are supposed to be home at a decent hour!' Their raised voices woke Meegan who promptly burst into tears.

'Now look what you've done!' Isla screamed at him.

'Me?' he asked in disbelief. With a huff, she stormed off into the living-room to comfort their daughter. Aiden shook his head wearily and drained his beer bottle.

Outside, dusk had settled in and shadows were fading fast. Soon it would be dark. Aiden enjoyed the dark void that came with night. When all colour was drained from the world, it felt as though the earth died, and each morning, with sunshine, she was reborn. A new start. Aiden's new start in Avalon wasn't going as well as he'd planned, but this was just the adapting period. Soon his family would feel more settled here and life would fall into a comfortable rhythm. For now, he was just riding out the storm of Isla's mood swings. He contemplated following her into the living-room and attempting to make up but he didn't see the point. He had done nothing wrong and wanted nothing more than to enjoy a deep, dreamless sleep. He headed upstairs to bed as Isla sat rocking Meegan back and forth, the little girl calm once more. When Aiden's head hit the pillow he left this world for another, and for eight blissful hours, everything felt perfect.

Chapter Eight

Unhappy Families

When Aiden awoke he found Isla curled up in bed beside him. He felt guilty about their argument the previous evening but decided against waking her. On his way downstairs he checked in on Meegan; she was still sound asleep, hugging her favorite stuff toy. As quietly as possible, he pottered about the kitchen, making himself some coffee and toast. Admittedly, he had gotten up earlier than usual. It was 7am and these days, he normally didn't have to be up until 8. Part of him knew that he was trying to avoid Isla. He knew that she would still be sore about their fight, especially since he went up to bed without first making-up with her. Whilst he didn't like arguing with his wife, he had bigger things on his mind. He was going to see Brandy that morning to finally find out what happened on that fateful night when she murdered her husband.

Aiden already had his own theory about what had transpired between them but he needed to hear it from Brandy. He was certain that she would be distressed recalling the details to him and he felt strangely disturbed by this. He should feel disconnected from his clients, an impassive observer just there to help perform legalities. Yet he felt involved with Brandy's case, perhaps because he felt that he was the only person who believed her, her only ally.

He filled his favorite blue mug up with black coffee and sat down at the table. It was silly how attached he was to the mug, but it held a lot of memories for him. Sometimes you needed to feel connected to the past.

It was a dull morning; the clouds were dense with the promise of rain. He momentarily toyed with the idea of waking Meegan but knew that it would only be for selfish reasons. He was feeling the weight of this case, and her smiling face and childish giggles would have been a welcome distraction. Isla, however, was just making him feel even worse about things. Wasn't a wife's duty to support her husband? No, that was an embarrassingly old-fashioned view. But still...he was the sole breadwinner in the house these days, yet she still moaned at him and pulled him apart. He had hoped that Avalon would have started to rub off on her by now. He didn't know what he had expected, perhaps a Stepford Wives-style transformation? Isla was still being difficult and it saddened him to think that rather than leave their problems in Chicago, they appeared to have followed them to Avalon. Perhaps he had been foolish to think that relocating the family would solve everything.

Movement upstairs disturbed Aiden from his thoughts. He hastily finished his coffee and left the house. As Isla entered the kitchen, rubbing the sleep from her eyes, she saw Aiden backing out of the driveway. She caught his eyes and he waved half-heartedly. She didn't bother returning the gesture.

'You're mighty eager today,' Brandy smiled as she sat down opposite Aiden. 'I've only just finished my breakfast!' His visits always brightened her day, but they weren't normally so early.

'What did you have?' Aiden asked, more to help make Brandy at ease than out of genuine interest. She made a face as if she was about to be sick.

'Porridge, eugh,' she made vomiting sounds. 'It looks like cement, it tastes like cement!'

'Sounds delicious!' he laughed.

'Well then, I'll make sure to save you some next time!'

As nice as it was to banter with Brandy, Aiden was there for a reason.

'Brandy.' She looked at him, eyes wide, face open, ready and willing to tell him whatever he needed to know.

'I need you to tell me what happened the night of April 16th.' He watched her closely, waiting for her to start crying or shaking, but to his surprise she remained calm.

'The night I killed Brandon?'

'Yes, that's the one.'

'Right you are then,' she coughed nervously. 'Well, I stabbed him.'

'I know you stabbed him. I need to know why you stabbed him. What happened that night to make you stab him?'

'What happened that night? You mean what had happened for the last five years? Each time he hit me, spat on me, called me names, that is what led up to that night. I was planning on leaving him. I'd saved up a bit of money, it wasn't much but it was enough to get me out of the state. My bag was all packed and ready by the door. I was determined to make a new start. He was supposed to be staying over at a friend's, but for some reason he came home.'

'How did he react when he knew you were leaving him?'

'Oh, you know, he gave me a kiss, said we had had a good run and wished me well,' she said sarcastically.

'How do you think he reacted?' Brandy's eyes darkened at the memory.

'He unleashed the devil's fury.'

'So he attacked you?'

Brandy squirmed in her chair, pained by the memories she was being forced to recall.

'Like I said, he came home early, all liquored up and horny as a schoolboy. He was all, 'Baby come to bed,' and I kept resisting but trying to keep him calm. Hoping against hope that he wouldn't spot my bag. At first he didn't. But his hands were all over me, I kept pushing him off but he wouldn't take no for an answer. It wasn't the first time he had forced himself on me, but I knew it was going to be the last, so after a while I just stopped fighting and let him have his fun. I was kind of banking on him falling asleep after anyways, and then I'd just leave whilst he was sleeping off his night of drinking. But after, as he was about to go and collapse on the bed, he noticed the bag out of the corner of his eye. Real calm, he turns to me and asks where I'm going. I start to panic, but try to seem all OK, so I tell him I've found my Ma after all these years and that I'm going to see her. He calls me a liar and punches me square in the face. Then he walks off into the other room and I'm hoping that he's done. But he comes back in with my ironing board and iron and sets them up, yelling that I've got chores to do before I can go anywhere.'

Brandy stops and starts rubbing her arms nervously.

'What happened?' Aiden hated himself for asking.

'He starts taking my clothes out of my bag, telling me that they are creased and need ironing. I don't know what to do so I just go along with it and start ironing, still thinking that if I keep him happy he'll leave me alone soon enough and I can escape. Then suddenly, halfway through, he grabs my one arm, holds it up and snatches the iron out of the other. He had a wild look in his eyes, like he'd lost all control. I tried to get away but he was too strong. He said that he knew I was going to leave him, but that I couldn't because of our vows. He said that we were together until death did us part. I was terrified, and then he...' she undid the zipper on her orange jumpsuit. The guards stepped forward to intervene but Aiden held up his hand to let them know it was OK. She wore a plain, white bra but he didn't see that. He couldn't take his eyes off her flat stomach and the three distinct iron shaped burns that covered it.

'The pain, it was so bad, I begged him to stop. When he was satisfied, he stormed out of the room and I just lay there in agony. I thought about calling the hospital but decided against it. I needed to get away. I dragged myself to my feet and started putting my clothes back in the bag. He came back in and slapped me so hard I fell against the ground. He spat on me, kicked me, called me an ungrateful whore. I was crying and pleading with him but his eyes were hollow, like he was a man possessed. I scrambled to my feet and he began throwing things at me, anything and everything. By now I was in the kitchen, holding on to the countertop for support. He's still chucking things, and while his back was momentarily turned I picked up the biggest knife in the drawer that I could find. I didn't have no intention of killing him, I just wanted to stop him from hurting me. But he noticed the knife. He came over, knocked me to the floor, the knife went flying, and wrapped his hands around my neck. I couldn't breathe, everything was going black. I knew that if I didn't do something I was going to die. With the last bit of strength that I had I reached across the floor, found the knife and then just plunged it into his bulk of a body as many times as it took for him to finally loosen his grip.'

Brandy shook her head in sadness and disbelief. Her arms hugged her tiny body as she struggled to find some comfort from her grief.

'So, you killed him in self-defense?' Aiden reasoned.

'But, I wanted him to die. After, he was so still, and there was blood everywhere. I didn't know what to do. I just watched him for a while, convinced that he wasn't dead, that the moment I turned my back he was going to get up and finish me off. I worked up enough courage to take a look into his eyes; they were glazed over, as if he were staring far, far into the distance, that was when I knew the devil had finally taken him. I called 911, I can't even remember what I said. It felt like the world was moving in slow motion, nothing felt real. I just sat there, waiting for the police to come, feeling nothing but relief to finally be free of Brandon.'

'Who turned up, was it sheriff Fern?'

'Sheriff Fern arrived at the house first. He took one look at Brandon, then at me covered in his blood and just handcuffed me straight away, no questions or anything. I was screaming and crying when he led me away, telling him that it wasn't my fault but he just looked me square in the eye and called me a demon. Two other officers showed up as he was putting me in his squad car. They paid me no mind, just went straight to gawk at Brandon's body.'

'Were you seen by a doctor, for your burns?'

'No, I tried to talk to Sheriff Fern as he drove me to the station but he just turned his radio up as high as it would go so as not to hear me. He is a cold man.'

'Yeah, he didn't strike me as the friendly type,' Aiden said as he furiously wrote notes. He glanced again at the copy he had of the police report from April 16th. It was noted that Brandy had been hysterical, but there was no mention of the wounds she had.

Again, it was signed off by sheriff Fern. The post-mortem merely stated that he had died from multiple stab wounds; it also noted that there had been a toxicology report. However, Aiden did not have those results. He had not noticed that they were missing before, yet he had no memory of having read them, which meant that Buck Fern had never given them to him.

'You said Brandon was drunk?'

'As an Irishman.'

Surely, Buck Fern would not go to such lengths just to disguise that Brandon was drunk. It was hardly a sin to drink too much. No, there must be something else.

'Did Brandon ever take drugs?'

'I don't think so.'

'But if he did, it may help to explain his violent behavior. You said he became a different person once you were married.'

'Yes, he completely changed.'

'If he did do drugs, that might help to explain that change.'

'I don't know, Mr. Connelly. Brandon took his health real serious. He still saw himself as an athlete, I couldn't see him taking no drugs.'

Aiden glanced at his watch.

'I'm afraid I'm going to have to leave you for today.' Brandy seemed deeply saddened by this.

'Well, thank you, Mr. Connelly. For taking the time to listen to me.'

'It is OK,' he felt himself blush. He wasn't used to this kind of genuine appreciation.

'You don't think I'm a monster, do you? I know what people have been saying and I'm not like that.'

'I don't think that you are a monster, Brandy. Far from it.'

'Good,' Brandy smiled. 'Because when you look at me, Mr. Connelly, for the first time in a long time, I feel like a person. Like what I say matters. And I'd hate it if you stopped looking at me like that.'

'I won't.'

'You are a good man.'

'I try to be.'

The guards led away Prisoner 929. To Aiden, she was no longer a murderer; he had never truly believed that she was capable of killing someone in cold blood. She was a victim of circumstance. If she hadn't killed Brandon, he would have undoubtedly killed her. But, if she were to die for her crime, would that be justice, or would it just be Brandon getting what he wanted, even from beyond the grave?

Aiden decided to go home for his lunch. He needed to clear his head and he was hoping to make things right with Isla. He hated it when they were arguing and he needed her support now more than ever. He entered the kitchen, full of optimism, smiling widely, but his wife met him with a cold, hard stare.

'Where the hell have you been?' her tone was accusing and she had her hands placed firmly on her hips.

'I've been at work, where do you think I've been?' his good intentions for a reconciliation were quickly evaporating. This wasn't the kind of welcome he had been hoping for.

'I called the office. You weren't there,' her eyes were locked on to his, simmering with rage. He wished he hadn't bothered coming home.

'Where's Meegan?' he asked, glancing around the kitchen, noticing that she wasn't there.

'Answer the question,' Isla's voice rose a notch, she was close to boiling point.

'Where's Meegan?' Aiden asked again, defying his wife.

'She's upstairs napping, now answer the goddamn question!' she was shouting now. He knew that he needed to calm her down or else she would wake their daughter.

'I was at the prison, working.'

'At the prison!'

'Yes, where my client is. For Christ's sake, Isla. Why are you being such a bitch?'

'I'm the bitch? Oh, that's rich!' her face was flushed with anger, her eyes still cold with fury.

'I'm not the one who stabbed my husband to death, and is now moving on to someone else's man!'

'What are you talking about?' Aiden just wanted to run out of the house and get some peace and quiet, but he knew that if he

114

didn't deal with his wife's anger now it would just be waiting for him, even more intensified, when he returned home.

'I'm talking about that little whore that you keep visiting at the prison!'

'What, Brandy?' he could not conceal the element of shock he felt at his wife's unreasonable aggression towards Brandy.

'Don't act all innocent, Aid. It won't wash. You are always at that stupid prison, seeing that wretched woman. Does she bat her eyes at you? Does she tell you that you are her only hope? Bet it makes you feel like some big strong man!'

'You are being completely ridiculous!' now he was shouting too. He hoped that for Meegan's sake she was managing to sleep through it all.

'Am I? Tell me, is she pretty?'

'What?'

'Tell me, Aid, is she attractive?'

'Well…yes,' he didn't have the energy to lie.

'I knew it!' Isla threw her hands up in the air and began to cry.

'Don't be so stupid! Just because she is attractive that doesn't mean I'm attracted to her! Grow up!'

'Lately, you are never here. You just come home to sleep! Do you have any idea how you are making me feel?'

'I'm trying, I am really trying, Isla, but you aren't making this any easier on either of us!'

'Did you even notice that I'd painted the living-room?'

Aiden remained silent, knowing that he'd failed to notice the change of colour on the walls of the living-room, but knew full well that this was not the time to admit that.

'Well, Aid, did you notice the fucking living-room or not?' she was yelling again, her face contorted with anger, her eyes bloodshot and wet with tears.

'No,' he said quietly and hung his head, waiting for the inevitable tidal wave of anguished screams and curse words which were about to wash over him.

'Do you even see me?' her voice was quiet which unnerved him. He was expecting anger and rage, but she had become oddly composed.

'You didn't notice my hair; more often than not you are too tired for sex. And now, you don't even give a shit about our home.'

'I do give a shit, I've just been…distracted.'

'By that whore!' the anger in his wife was rising again.

'It's not like that. It is a difficult case.'

'No, it isn't Aiden. She killed her husband, she is guilty. What is difficult about that?'

'There's more to it, I know it!' he slammed his fist against the table in frustration.

'She is just a manipulative monster who has got you wrapped around her little finger!'

In her anger, and full of spite, Isla grabbed Aiden's faithful, blue mug from the side. The mug which meant so much to him, which he had drunk from time and again, that he had loved for so many years. She took the mug in her hand and in one swift movement, threw it at the wall just beyond Aiden's head. He heard it whirl past before the ceramic smashed against the wall and shattered. He heard each shard fall to the ground, destroyed. He didn't turn to view the massacre; he didn't want to give his wife the satisfaction of a reaction.

'You have no idea what you are talking about!' Aiden roared, his mind no longer worrying about disturbing Meegan, instead pushed to the limit by his wife's constant bickering. He strode over to her, full of purpose and angry intent. He placed his face so close to hers that their noses were almost touching. Isla cowered in fear, she had never seen her husband this mad before; she knew that she had taken things too far.

'You are a self-involved bitch who has no idea what she is talking about,' he hissed.

With that, he turned on his heel and marched out of the kitchen without looking back.

'Aid,' Isla cried after him, sobbing. 'Aid, please.'

But her cries were in vain, he was already gone. He had taken all he could from his wife for the day. He'd probably pick up some flowers on the way home to help smooth things over, but for now he needed to get away. Brandy was due to stand trial for murder in a week; he knew that he had to do something, and fast.

Isla stood alone, weeping. The remains of what was once the blue mug looked up at her, a painful metaphor of her marriage. Did she pick up the pieces and try to mend something so badly broken, or did she simply toss it out with the trash and replace it? As she stood there, in a strange town, feeling abandoned by the man she had sworn to love for the rest of her life, she had no idea what to do.

'Aiden, are you sure that you have thought this through?' Edmond's face was pale and worried.

'Yes, Edmond, I'm really sure.'

'It's just,' he sighed deeply, 'you are new to town, you are only just starting to get to know people. If you choose to do this, on your head be it. I'll play no part in any of it.'

'You won't have to.'

'I'm sorry but I can't be involved at all, I hope that you understand.'

Aiden understood; the moment he had told Edmond Copes of his plans the portly man had turned ashen. He had closed the blinds and sent Betty out for coffee, even though there was plenty. It all seemed extremely cloak and dagger.

'What you are proposing to do, it will upset a lot of very important people,' he was whispering, fearful.

'I've no doubt. But I wouldn't do anything without running it past you first.'

'I'm glad that you did but you must be prepared. Once news gets out, people will be angry, you must expect a fair amount of backlash.' Aiden was already aware of what to expect; he knew that many people, such as Buck Fern, would relish any excuse to be hostile towards him.

'But what makes you so sure? How do you know that she isn't lying? I've learned to never trust a beautiful woman. The more plain a lady is, the less lies that she can get away with.'

'I believe her,' and Aiden did. He believed in her so much that he was willing to sacrifice his reputation, possibly even his career.

'It is just hard to take in. Brandon…a wife beater?' Edmond shook his head.

'He was always such a nice lad. I knew that he liked a drink or two, but then who doesn't?' At that moment, after Aiden had delivered his shocking decision to him, Edmond needed a drink more than ever to steady his nerves. His mind was racing as he worried about Avalon's reaction. What if his offices were vandalized? What if he himself were attacked?

'Is your case solid?'

'Solid enough,' Aiden was confident with his evidence. 'There are just a few holes that I need to sort out, but it is nothing much.'

'I just hope she is telling the truth, for your sake.' Edmond was genuinely concerned for the young lawyer. He had seen Brandy White; she was the most dangerous type of beautiful in his eyes. She didn't lure you into bed with hungry eyes and moist lips; instead she found a way into your heart, with her soft features and angelic nature. She was the sort of woman who, if she said the sky was green, you'd believe her. He was fearful that she had worked her magic on Aiden. Edmond berated himself for not having handled the case himself. He felt as if he were feeding Aiden to the lions, and try as he might the young man was hell-bent on self-destruction it would seem.

'It might not even work,' Edmond tried another tact; planting doubt in Aiden's mind.

'It has to. She can't die for this.'

'You are young, stubborn and idealistic. But surely, from your work in the city, you have seen that the law is far from black and white?'

'I've had some tough cases, but this - I can do something, I can help. I have to do something, Edmond. If I didn't, I could never live with myself.'

'And if she still dies?'

'Then at least I tried.' Aiden was full of courage and optimism, qualities which had long left Edmond, and he admired the young man. If only he could see what trouble he was about to unleash upon himself. But if it were true, if Brandon had beaten Brandy, what good would that information do now? He was dead, nothing could change that. But these allegations would hurt those he had left behind, who were still raw and grieving for him.

Aiden could sense how uneasy Edmond was.

'I will not speak of this again to you. It is my decision, and any backlash that comes from it is mine to deal with,' he tried to calm his colleague's nerves.

'Then, I'll let you get on with it. You need to alert the courts that this is no longer a murder trial. That you will be attempting to have Brandy White tried for manslaughter.'

Hearing it aloud made Aiden all the more certain that he was doing the right thing. If Brandy was found guilty of manslaughter, under federal law, she would serve a life sentence, rather than have her life ended if she had committed murder. Brandon's death had not been preordained, it was a crime of passion, and anyone in Brandy's position would have done the same thing. He knew that the people of Avalon would not welcome the revelation that their beloved hero was a monster behind closed doors but the truth needed to come out. In his line of work, too often Aiden had seen guilty men walk free because fear kept their victims silent. The only way to end abuse, suffering, was to speak up. Brandon would lose his halo, but perhaps the town would stop vilifying Brandy and just realize, as he had, that she was just a kind, loving woman, driven to do something awful.

In a small town, news travels alarmingly fast. It wasn't always a good idea to be the bearer of bad news, but sometimes, standing by and not saying anything can land you in even more trouble. Edmond waited until Aiden had left and he had heard his car drive away; with a heavy heart he picked up his phone and dialed. He knew how things worked in Avalon, he knew that it was important to keep friends in high places.

'Clyde, hello,' he said as the other end of the line picked up.

'I'm afraid I've got some bad news regarding Brandy's case...'

Chapter Nine

Don't Be Fooled

Aiden had anticipated that once news got round that he was going to try and change Brandy's plea to manslaughter people would be unhappy. Perhaps even downright rude to him. He was standing at the gas station, filling up his car, and could feel numerous pairs of eyes boring into his back. When he looked around, familiar faces who normally greeted him with a smile either looked away in disgust or gave him a stony glare. He told himself that in time their anger would subside, but he was hurt by their attitude.

When he stopped to grab a coffee, the attendant was brisk, and when he turned his back to leave the young guy clearly called Aiden a dick. He was trying to rise above it, to remember that all these people who were so quick to cast stones didn't know the whole story like he did. He did wonder how they could already know about the intricacies of the case, but he didn't dwell on it for too long. He was quickly learning that in a town as close knit as Avalon, news travels faster than fire.

As Aiden came into Cope and May Attorneys at Law he found himself wishing his day away. He wanted nothing more than the cruel whispering and the hateful looks to stop. It was like being back in high school. A place that had seemed so friendly and welcoming now appeared vicious and segregated. He hoped that in his workplace he would find a sanctuary from the accusing eyes and harsh tongues. He was wrong.

'Morning, Betty,' he greeted her with all the cheer that he could muster.

'Mr. Connelly,' her tone was cold; she didn't even look up from her computer to acknowledge him. He sighed with disappointment and went into the office.

'Oh, Mr. Connelly,' Betty called after him. Aiden hoped that perhaps she was going to apologize, say that she was just caught up in the combined mentality of the town and didn't mean to be rude to him. He looked at her in hope.

'Mr. Copes won't be in today, he is sick.'

'No,' Aiden thought to himself, 'he is hiding.' He knew how bad the aftermath of Aiden's decision would be and had wisely chosen to ride out the storm at home.

He shut himself in his office, thankful to be alone. He toyed with asking Betty for a coffee, but decided against it.

When people believed that he was going to help send Brandy to her death, they admired him. Now that he was sticking his neck out to save her life he was being vilified. Brandon had truly managed to brainwash all those around him. The truth of it was that no one wanted to accept that Brandon, who they held in such high regard, was violent and abusive, because of the implication it meant for them. It would mean that an entire town turned a blind eye as an innocent woman was constantly beaten, and that would make them bad people. To witness an injustice and not speak out is almost as bad as committing the wrongdoing. If Brandon had done all the terrible things that Brandy had said he had, it meant that Avalon wasn't this close, loving community it tried to portray itself as. It would all be a lie. It would mean that it was as cold and as lonely a place to live in as any big city. Aiden was threatening to not only tarnish Brandon's image, but also the entire towns. It was little wonder that they now hated him so much.

Isla Connelly was doing her best to adapt to small town life. She was accustomed to cocktail parties, designer clothes stores and sushi restaurants. The only thing the people of Avalon seemed to keep manicured were their lawns. She felt like she was on another planet rather than just in another state. She missed her friends, she missed her penthouse, and she missed dry martinis and massages. But most of all she missed herself. Ever since they moved she felt that as each day passed a small part of her faded away. Social events now consisted of high school football games and church instead of hitting the town with the girls or dining out on the finest cuisine. But she knew why she was here. Aiden was becoming a stranger; she had felt it for a long time. It got to the point where she no longer knew how he took his coffee because he was never around long enough for her to make him one. Rather than become a statistic, they had packed their bags and turned their back on their old life, hoping to make a fresh start and learn from the mistakes that they had been making. But Isla knew all too well that old habits die hard. Her fights with Aiden were breaking her heart yet she couldn't help but lash out at him. As stupid as she knew it was, she was jealous of Brandy White. She needed her husband to support her, instead he was off helping a murderer. Yet in her heart she still knew him enough to know that if he were fighting so very hard for Brandy that he must have sensed that there was something there worth fighting for. Aiden had his faults, but he was a sincere, kind and loving man. He was the last of a dying breed. This was why Isla painted on her smile with lipstick, as she did each day, and took Meegan out in her stroller, determined not to give up.

It was a pleasant enough day as she pushed her daughter along the street. She wanted to make things right with Aiden so she was heading to the small grocery store in the town centre to pick up a few essentials to cook him a special dinner.

'What shall we make for Daddy's dinner tonight?' she asked Meegan, who was currently entranced by the pinwheel she was holding, watching with glee as it blew in the gentle breeze.

'Mashed potato!' she yelled excitedly.

'We can't just give Daddy mashed potato! He needs a proper dinner.'

'Squirrel!'

'Ick, can't cook him squirrel, silly.' Then she noticed, from Meegan's outstretched hand pointing, that 'squirrel' had been an observation rather than a suggestion. Isla laughed to herself. There was an abundance of wildlife in Avalon, something which they didn't have in the city, unless you counted cockroaches and rats. Meegan adored watching butterflies in the garden or listening to crickets at night. Isla was even toying with the idea of taking the little girl horse riding when she was a bit older. Isla had always wanted a horse, and now perhaps she would be able to have one.

With the sun on her back and the clean air in her lungs, Isla was finally starting to feel as though she was settling into country life. As she navigated the stroller through the doorway of the grocery store she was greeted with a smile by Andy, the elderly owner. She waved and began wandering the few aisles, collecting what she needed. She hooked her basket to the back of the stroller to stop Meegan loading it up with random goods. However, this didn't stop the little girl, as when Isla looked down to check on her she was holding a box of crackers, a jar of peaches and a packet of spaghetti.

'Oh, Meegan,' she despaired, removing the items and trying to find their appropriate location on the shelves.

'What has Mommy told you about picking things up in shops?' Meegan just laughed as her mother scolded her and started reaching out for more treasures. 'Stop that!' Isla pushed the stroller into the centre of the aisle so that Meegan couldn't reach any of the items.

'Kids can sure be tricky,' a male voice from behind her noted.

'Yes, they can be very tricky,' Isla said, turning around. She was greeted by a tall man; she guessed late fifties by the lines on his face and the grey in his hair. He was devilishly handsome though; even more so as he was wearing a pale blue shirt which was unbuttoned enough to hint at an admirable physique.

'Oh, hello, I don't think we've met. I'm Isla Connelly,' she offered him her hand and blushed profusely when he kissed the back of it in a gentlemanly manner.

'Lovely to meet you. I believe I've met your husband.'

'Aiden?'

'Yes, indeed. Allow me to introduce myself. My name is Clyde White, I run the local timber company, Avalon Pine.'

White. A glimmer of recognition ran through Isla's mind; it only toOK a few seconds for her to realize where she had heard that name before and a shiver ran down her spine.

'So you have lived in Avalon for a long time?' she attempted to make small talk, not wanting the conversation to turn towards the murder trial.

'Yes, a very long time. I have some very dear friends in this town, very loyal friends.' She didn't like his tone, it sounded slightly menacing.

'You and your family moved here recently I gather?'

'Yes, that's right.' She was beginning to feel nervous.

'I expect you will be wanting to make good friends too. So it is important to stay on the right side of people, don't you think?'

'Yes, yes of course.' She placed her hands behind her upon the handle bar of the stroller in case she felt the need to make a swift exit.

'You and your husband seem like a lovely couple. It would be a shame to get off on the wrong foot.'

'Yes, it would,' Isla was confused as to what Clyde White was trying to imply. 'Why would we be getting off on the wrong foot?'

'Well, my dear, you must surely know that your husband is representing the woman who murdered my son.'

'Yes, I do.' Isla had been hoping that Brandy would not be mentioned. 'I'm awfully sorry, for the loss of your son,' she quickly added.

'He was a fine man,' Clyde seemed wistful for a moment. 'Does your husband discuss the case with you at all?' he snapped back to the situation at hand.

'No, not really,' Isla was saddened by the admission, wishing that Aiden did share more with her.

'Shame. I was hoping that you could help him see sense.'

'See sense?'

'He hasn't told you?'

'Told me what?'

'He is going to try and have that murdering witch tried for manslaughter because she has told him wicked lies about my son and he has fallen for them. As any red-blooded man would. She is a true beauty, my poor Brandon was long held under her spell.'

Isla prickled at the mention of Brandy's beauty. She was already feeling sore about how much time Aiden was spending with her.

'I know my son; he never laid a finger on her. It would be in your family's best interest to change his mind.' Clyde White took a step towards Isla. She tightened her grip on the stroller, and from the corner of her eye saw that Andy was no longer at the checkout, he had gone into the back room for something. She was alone with the very angry father of Brandon.

'I'll talk to him.'

'Good,' Clyde smiled. He looked past her and saw Meegan playing happily with her pinwheel.

'Is that your daughter? She is lovely.'

'Thank you,' Isla just wanted to leave.

'It would be an awful shame if something were to happen to her.' She starred at Clyde in horror; his eyes were now dark and menacing.

'There is nothing worse than losing a child, trust me. I suggest you take good care of her.' Isla nodded and dashed out of the store.

She was almost running with the stroller, desperate to get home and lock the door behind her. It was only in the safety of the kitchen did she notice that she had left without paying for her groceries but she was too scared to go back.

Alone in the office, Aiden was listening to his own thoughts. In the empty silence around him he was beginning to wonder if he was doing the right thing. He was jeopardizing his life in Avalon, but surely if he ultimately saved a life it was all worth it.

'Mr. Connelly?' Betty's voice through the intercom startled him.

'Yes, Betty?' he replied, hoping that her anger had now subsided and she was enquiring as to whether he would like a coffee. He was longing for a drink, his throat felt like sandpaper.

'You have a visitor.' It wasn't the response he had been hoping for.

'Who is it?'

'Sheriff Buck.' Aiden's heart sank even further. He hesitated for a moment, debating making up some kind of excuse as to why he couldn't see the old man. He knew why he was here, to challenge on him on his decision to change Brandy's plea. Aiden was in mood to fight her cause at that very moment; the court room was the place to defend her integrity, and his own, not the office.

'Mr. Connelly?'

'Send him in,' he sighed.

Buck Fern did not need words to convey how he his feeling, his face said it all for him. He regarded Aiden with a mixture of disgust and contempt. He sat down opposite the young lawyer, still not speaking. Aiden humored the sheriff for a while but then decided that enough was enough.

'Can I help you, Sheriff Fern?' He shot Aiden a glance filled with spite.

'I just came here to talk with you, man to man.'

'Very well, let's talk then.'

It was the first time since meeting Sheriff Fern that Aiden had seen him appear out of his depth. His old eyes, although angry, were searching helplessly around the room.

'I just want to know why,' his gaze at last settled on Aiden as he spoke.

'Why what?' he knew full well what Buck was referring to but asked him all the same.

'Why you are choosing to drag a good man's name through the mud?'

'I'm not. By all accounts, Brandon was far from a good man.'

'How dare you!' Buck was enraged. 'You didn't know him! You have no right to say that! You are just listening to the cheap lies of an evil little witch who would say anything right now to save her own skin!'

'Calm down, Sheriff Fern, I thought you came here to talk, not shout.'

Buck Fern exhaled deeply, calming himself. He would have loved nothing more than to wrap Aiden's tie around his neck until his face went purple. But he had to remain calm; he had to convince this outsider to change his mind.

'You have no proof, only her word.'

'What makes you say that?'

The old man was silent.

'Well, I suppose since you tried to cover up Brandon's crimes, you would think that I had no proof. But even you can't hide everything.'

'You have nothing.'

'The police reports and the hospital files speak for themselves. Brandy doesn't even have to utter a word for the jury to see, without a doubt, that Brandon abused her.' Aiden was bluffing; he had evidence, true, but nothing concrete as yet. However, his bluff seemed to work as Sheriff Fern seemed agitated.

'Like I said, you got nothing. Brandon never got in no trouble with the law.'

'Because you always turned up on the scene first to smooth things over. Why did you protect him?'

Silence.

'Was Clyde White paying you to keep his son's indiscretions quiet?'

'You don't know what you are doing,' Sheriff Fern said softly. 'If you want to stay in this town, I suggest you drop your current line of enquiry and just do things by the book.'

'Are you threatening me?'

Silence.

'I won't be intimidated by the threats of an old, corrupt sheriff. Brandon White routinely abused his young wife to the point where she had no choice but to take his life. Before this case is over I will see to it that the whole of Avalon knows what a monster he was.'

'You are young and full of fire, I respect that. But you are also gullible to the ways of a beautiful woman. She is lying to you. I don't blame you for being taken in by her; she has a mighty pretty face, like that of an angel. But, even angels fall, Mr. Connelly. She is the devil and you best believe it.'

'You were there, the night Brandon glassed her. Why didn't you do anything?'

Buck Fern ran his hand over his face in thought.

'Why do you persist on doing this? Let the dead be in peace.'

'But Brandy isn't dead! You saw what he did to her and yet you did nothing!'

'What goes on between a husband and wife is their business.'

'So you admit that he beat her?'

'No! I'm saying that I answered the 911 call, when I get there she was all cut up, so I send her over to the hospital to get sorted out. Young couples full of passion are always arguing.'

'Would you ever strike a woman?'

'No!'

'Well, you are acting as though you condone it.'

'You need to leave it be.'

Aiden could see that Sheriff Fern was beginning to crack; in the old man's anguish he was releasing snippets of information which could prove vital. He had to seize the opportunity.

'Did Brandon have a drinking problem?'

'Not that I'm aware of.'

'He had a few DUIs, was cautioned a few times for being drunk and disorderly. Sounds like he had a drinking problem to me.'

'Everyone likes to go out and have a few drinks, let loose. Nothing wrong with that. Sometimes he took it too far but he was young, all young guys are like that.'

'The toxicology report from his post-mortem is missing.'

'There wasn't one.'

'It is common procedure to conduct a toxicology report. Where is his? Are you withholding it from me? If you are I will get a warrant to search your offices!'

'I'm not withholding anything. There wasn't one.'

'Why? Did you stop it? Was he high when he attacked Brandy? Was he doing drugs?'

'Why can't you accept that he was a decent man?'

'If he was such a decent man, why would his wife kill him?'

'She is mental, Connelly! Evil, driven by spite. You are meant to help deliver justice, stop her killing another man again, not try and destroy the memory of Brandon.'

Sheriff Fern rose to his feet.

'I believe that we are done here.'

Aiden also stood and offered the old man his hand; to his surprise he shook it.

'If you take this to court, people will hate you,' Buck said shaking his hand. 'Whatever she says Brandon did, or didn't do, to everyone here he was a hero. And he is the one who was stabbed, not her. She is still here. He didn't deserve to die so why does she deserve to live?'

'I don't think that she does deserve to die.'

'It is not our place to decide who should live and who should die. It is the Lord's.'

Sheriff Fern left the offices of Cope and May Attorneys at Law disheartened. Aiden Connelly was a more stubborn man than he had bargained for. Brandy White's fate would be decided in court; Buck Fern could only hope that justice would be served.

Aiden came home to find Isla sat nursing a glass of red wine at the kitchen table. Her eyes were stained red from crying. He placed the flowers he had bought for her on his way home down and went over to comfort his wife.

'Baby, I'm sorry I've been so busy with work,' he rubbed her back soothingly. Isla took a sip from her wine glass as fresh tears began to slide down her cheeks.

'It isn't that, Aid,' her voice was hoarse.

'Then what is it?' he slid into the chair next to her and cupped her hand in his. 'I bought you flowers,' he said weakly, just in case she was still mad with him. She looked over at the flowers momentarily and smiled sadly.

'They are beautiful, thank you.'

'Isla, what's wrong?'

'I went shopping today with Meegan.'

'Oh, well that's good, hon. Where is Meegan?'

'She's sleeping. We went to pick up some groceries. I wanted to make you something special for tea, but when we were there we ran into Clyde White.'

Aiden tensed. The last thing he wanted was his family being dragged into the circus that now surrounded Brandy's case.

'What did he say to you?'

'He threatened me!' Isla was crying profusely, her hands shaking.

'He what?!' Aiden could barely contain himself. 'What did he say?'

Isla was still crying and shaking, struggling to get her words out.

'Baby, calm down and tell me exactly what he said.' Obeying her husband she drank some more wine to try and steady herself.

'He said...he told me to look after Meegan.'

'Well, hun, that sounds more like advice than a threat.' He started to relax, concluding that as usual his wife was overreacting. He reasoned that she was perhaps putting on this whole charade to make him feel guilty about their argument.

'No, Aid, it was how he said it! He was really menacing, saying how awful it was to lose a child.'

'Well, he has lost a child. I'm sure you just misinterpreted what he meant.'

'No!' she was starting to get angry now. 'He was trying to scare me! He asked me to talk to you about the case, to try and get you to change your mind.'

'If that's the case, he is being unreasonable, I'll talk to him.'

131

'That won't help, Aid. Don't you see? You are turning everyone against us! This has to end!'

Aiden hung his head in shame. He had bought his troubles at work on to his own doorstep. He should have known just how low people would be willing to sink in order to preserve Brandon's memory. But he expected more from Clyde White. He had clearly misjudged the businessman.

'Why have you changed the plea? I don't understand!'

'Because it wasn't murder. It was a crime of passion. She doesn't deserve to die for what she did; I can't stand by and let her be persecuted for a crime she had no choice but to commit.'

'No, you said yourself it was open, shut!'

'Well, it isn't.'

'Why, Aid, are you doing this? Why do you have to put your ass on the line for this woman? She's sitting in jail where no one can get to her while you're putting your family in danger! This needs to end; you ARE going to try her for murder!'

'No, I'm not.'

'Yes!' Isla screamed hysterically. 'You are not going to put your family through hell after we have moved heaven and earth to do as you please!'

'I can't let her die.'

'Why not, she killed him didn't she?'

'Yes, but...'

'There is no but, Aiden. She did it, end of. Why do you insist on making this so difficult? Do you really think that he hit her? Or do you think that she is just trying to save her own skin?'

'I think that he hit her.'

'Well, maybe she deserved it,' Isla said spitefully, rage surging through her body.

'That is a vile thing to say, even for you.' Aiden replied in disgust.

'Do you ever stop to think why people are defending Brandon so intently? You never knew him; all you are hearing is one side of the story. He was clearly a good man who didn't deserve to die. You are being taken in by that bitch's lies!'

'But they aren't lies.'

132

'Yes, Aiden, they are,' she stood up, wine glass in hand.

'And now, because of what an idiot you have been, I have people threatening me, threatening our daughter! If you don't care about protecting me at least give a damn about her! I don't feel safe here anymore!'

'You're safe. Clyde White is just trying to scare you, to get to me,' Aiden hoped his words were true. He needed Isla to believe him; he needed her to calm down.

'No. You are going to change the plea or else so help me, I'll leave you! I'll walk, Aiden! And I'll take Meegan with me! Are you going to risk losing it all just to stop some little slut from getting what she deserves?' She wobbled slightly on her feet as she yelled at him.

'You've been drinking, we will talk about this another time,' he took the wine glass from her hand and tossed the remaining crimson liquid down the sink.

Isla's eyes gleamed with tears and fury.

'This has to end, Aid.'

'And it will.'

'I don't want to lose you over this,' she broke down and fell into his arms. He held her close, feeling her tears soak through his shirt and on to his skin. He hated doing this to her, but he had to stand firm. Clyde White was using dirty, sneaky tactics. Aiden wouldn't sink so low, he could only hope that the evidence would speak for itself once they were in the courtroom.

'Do you really think that her life is worth saving?' she looked up at her husband, her anger starting to subside.

'Baby, any life is worth saving.'

'I hope you are right.' Aiden knew he was right. He had consulted his conscience time and again over Brandy White and had decided to follow his gut instinct. Only time would tell if he had made the right decision.

As he held his wife, standing there in the kitchen of their new home, he prayed that Brandon had hit Brandy. Because if he hadn't, and if he had been foolish enough to believe the lies of a desperate woman, there was no telling what lengths Clyde White and Buck Fern would go to.

Chapter Ten

Father, Can You Hear Me?

When Brandy White saw Father West sitting on the opposite side of the Perspex glass her heart soared and an unfamiliar feeling began to creep up inside her. It was hope.

'Oh, Father West,' she gushed, leaning forward and pressing her palms against the glass.

'I knew you would come!'

Father West smiled fondly at her. Her love for him, for the church, was so sweet and pure. To see her like this, caged like an animal, it broke his heart.

'How are you doing, Brandy?'

'I'm doing OK, the food isn't all that great and I am getting mighty bored just sitting in my room all day long,' she spoke as if she were on a less than pleasant vacation, rather than sat on death row awaiting sentencing. He admired her courage, or was she merely in denial?

'The trial is only a few days away now. How are you feeling about it?'

'I'm feeling really good,' she smiled. 'I've been talking to Mr. Connelly; he has been so nice to me.'

'What have you told him?'

'I've told him…you know…what happened? And he didn't judge me, he was actually quite kind!'

'Well, he's a nice man.'

'Father West, I don't want people to hate me anymore. If they knew the truth about Brandon, about what he did, do you think they might understand me more?'

'I'm sure they will, Brandy.'

She smiled and her face lit up and Patrick West remembered, regretfully, the vows he had taken when joining the priesthood. He was still a flesh and blood man and when a woman as beautiful as Brandy smiled so fondly at him he began to have yearnings, desires. If it wasn't for the dog collar around his neck he would have taken her in his arms a long time ago and shown her how a real man loves a woman. But this was neither the time nor the place for such thoughts.

'You understand what will happen at the trial if you are found guilty?' he put the question to her as delicately as he could.

'I am guilty.'

'Well, yes, so you are aware of what will happen?'

'I'll die.' It seemed so surreal to hear her say those words. She was a healthy young woman, in the prime of her life, yet she was being forced to contemplate her impending fate. Her time on this earth was going to be cut tragically short.

'Have you made your peace with God?' he asked, hiding behind the priest mask. She nodded solemnly.

'I pray every night, asking Him to understand the choices I have made and to welcome me into His kingdom.'

'Good girl, remember, the Lord forgives all sins as long as you repent.' He felt like a fraud as he sat there facing her. Yes, in theory God forgave those who repented their sins, but what about those who commit murder? If you take another life what fate does await you on the other side? There was no guarantee that being sorry was enough to get you past the gates of heaven.

'Just make sure you keep praying, and I'll pray for you too.'

'Thank you, Father.'

They were both silent for a moment, each lost in their own thoughts. It was Brandy who spoke first, her voice unsteady,

'Am I...am I doing the right thing?'

'Of course you are,' he reached forward to touch her, forgetting the glass which kept them apart. His hand made a hollow sound as it smacked against it.

'Brandy, what you are doing is incredibly brave. The way that Brandon treated you…it was just disgusting. The town needs to know who he truly was. It sickens me when people celebrate him. He was a monster, a monster which you slyed. It should be you who is the hero!'

'I'd love that more than anything.'

'Love what?'

'To be seen as a hero. For people to look at me and smile. When I walk past people would just say hello instead of pointing and whispering behind my back. I'd give anything just to feel loved, just once. Like how everyone looked at me when I won my crown,' she bowed her head in sadness; the time when she could hold her head high with pride felt like an all too distant memory.

'You are a hero to me,' Father West tried to comfort her. But it was true; he did see her as a hero. She had conquered her demons and was accepting the consequences with such dignity and grace. He admired her more than she would ever know. Perhaps in another life, another time, he could have told her, he could have loved her.

'I'm so glad that you came. I was scared that you were going to desert me.'

'I could never desert you.'

'I want people to remember me as a good person but I know that they won't,' the thought that the eternal memory that the world would hold of her was to be a negative one left Brandy distraught. Sat day after day in her tiny cell at Eastham Ladies Penitentiary she had nothing but time to think, to re-evaluate her life. To relive mistakes over and over again. Her greatest regret was letting her mother go. She missed her dearly, even if she wasn't the greatest parent in the world. Now more than ever she could use her guidance, just a few kind words. Would Janice Cotton ever know that her daughter had died? Perhaps she would sense it, in only the way a mother could. That something that was once so close to you, so connected, was now gone forever. Maybe she would just wake up and feel a profound sense of emptiness, like something was missing but she couldn't work out what. As long as on some level she knew that her daughter had passed, Brandy would be happy.

Father West hated to leave Brandy there, alone, but he had no choice.

'I'm afraid I must go, I have service in an hour.'

'Yes, of course.'

'I'll be thinking of you.'

'Will you come again?'

He knew he shouldn't. This one visit was already tearing him up inside more than he had imagined it would.

'I'll try to,' he lied.

'Remember me,' she said softly as she was led away, tears pricking at her eyes. The greatest fear that anyone dying young had to face was remembrance. That in their all too brief time on Earth they had failed to leave any lasting mark. But Brandy White would be remembered. Perhaps not for the right reasons, but her name would be on the lips of the people of Avalon for many years to come.

'Mommy, where we going?' Meegan asked as Isla strapped the toddler into her car seat.

'We are going to see one of Daddy's friends', she told her as she consulted her map once more.

'Why isn't Daddy coming?'

'Daddy is working, baby girl. It is just you and me,' the words echoed in her head long after she had said them. Avalon no longer felt remotely like home. Isla felt like the townspeople were watching her every move, judging her. If Aiden didn't change his plea, their family would be forever branded. She couldn't have that. If they were to remain there, then for Meegan's sake, she had to do something. As she drove off she wondered if she was doing the right thing, but Aiden had left her with no other option.

'You sure are popular today,' the guard said as she opened up Prisoner 929's cell.

'What?' Brandy asked, confused.

'You've got another visitor.'

137

Her heart soared as she was led into the familiar visiting room with the glass wall. She was expecting to see Aiden sat there waiting for her, but to her surprise she was confronted by a woman. Not just a woman, but also a child. A small girl was sat on the woman's knee, gazing out at Brandy with terrified eyes. For a moment Prisoner 929 hesitated. Clearly, this visitor was not for her; she had never seen her before in her life.

'My, you truly are stunning,' the woman said to her sadly. Bemused, Brandy sat down in her chair.
'It is no wonder that he comes to see you so much.'
'I'm sorry but do I know you?'
'No, but you know my husband.'
'Your husband?'
'Yes, Aiden Connelly, your lawyer. He is my husband.'

As Brandy took in the identity of her female visitor, Isla watched her intently. She was breathtaking. With youth on her side and a glowing mane of luscious blonde hair she was the stuff of every teenage boy's fantasy. Isla watched for any hint of guilt in her eyes, or shame, but if anything, she seemed frightened. Sat behind the glass, Mrs. Connelly was beginning to feel extremely foolish for having come. There was no way Aiden could be having any sort of physical relationship with this young woman, he couldn't even touch her! She was stupid to have ever entertained the idea that he had feelings for the girl. Yet here she was; she had to say something.

'I wanted to come and see you.'
Meegan leant forward, intrigued by the wall of glass, and began placing her little hands all over it.
'Is that your daughter?'
'Yes, it is,' Isla wrapped an arm around Meegan protectively and realized that it was not just Brandy who was afraid. The reality that she had brought her infant child to a prison and was now exposing her to a killer was beginning to sink in. In her crazed jealous rage she had thought only of confronting Brandy, not the impact it may have on her child.

138

'She is lovely,' Brandy placed a hand against Meegan's on the glass and the little girl giggled. 'Why did you bring her here? It isn't the best place for a child.'

'I thought that if you saw her, saw me…us, you might change your mind.'

'Change my mind? Mrs. Connelly, I don't follow you?'

'You've told my husband that you killed, Brandon isn't it, because he beat you. And now, Aiden wants to change your plea from murder to manslaughter. I'm sure you are already aware of all this.'

Brandy remained quiet, still trying to understand why Aiden's wife had come to see her.

'Well, people in town aren't happy. Just the other day, Clyde White, well, he threatened me and my daughter.'

'He did?' Brandy cried. 'That pompous pig of a man!'

'Yes, well, if you are still tried for murder, as you were meant to be, he will leave me and my family alone.'

'So what are you saying?'

'I'm saying that you may well have wrapped my husband round your little finger and got him to believe your lies but you are not fooling anyone else. Tell him that you lied, that Brandon never laid a hand on you and be tried for murder.'

'But I'm not lying!' Brandy protested.

'I don't care if you are lying or not. You are putting my family in danger. What difference does it make? If, you are tried for manslaughter, you will just spend the rest of your life rotting in a jail cell, is that what you want?'

'So, you are saying that my life doesn't matter?'

'Not as much as my daughter's life, no!'

Meegan was still placing her hands along the glass wall, giggling softly to herself. Brandy watched her with sad eyes.

'How old is she?'

'Two.'

'My baby would be nearly three,' her eyes welled up with tears as she continued to watch Meegan.

'You have a baby?' Isla asked, surprised.

'No, I lost my baby.'

'I'm sorry.'

'No you're not.'

139

Isla was taken aback by Brandy's abrupt reply.

'I understand that you want to protect your daughter, but to bring her here, to tell me to lie just because Clyde White spooked you. You are so very different to your husband.'

Brandy was now looking intently at Aiden's wife. She was pretty but not stunning. Her face seemed to be permanently contorted into a scowl which suggested that she wasn't exactly a ray of sunshine.

'Mr. Connelly is a good, decent man. He is kind and has only ever been nice to me. I find it hard to believe that he would be married to such a cruel, cold woman.'

'Don't you dare judge me!' Isla spat. Meegan cowered at her mother's angry tone and abruptly stopped playing with the glass and sat very still.

'You are telling me to put aside my own life for the sake of yours!'

'I didn't kill my husband, you did. You deserve everything you get.' The harsh words came tumbling out of Isla's mouth before she had chance to stop them.

'I bet you fit in real well in Avalon, Mrs. Connelly. You are just as hollow as the rest of them.'

'I'll be leaving now,' Isla stood up and grabbed Meegan.

'It was so lovely to meet you,' Brandy said sarcastically.

She watched Mrs. Connelly and her daughter leave, her mind wrapped up in what might have been. That could have been her, holding her own child. Yet now she would never have the chance to be a mother. Even the wife of the man she looked to as her savior wanted her dead. Perhaps the world would be a better place without her. Holding back tears, Brandy was led back to her cell, thankful for the first time to be alone.

Isla sat with her hands on the wheel in the parking lot of Eastham Ladies Penitentiary. Beside her, Meegan had quickly got over the drama in the interview room and was sleeping soundly in her car seat. She was disturbed by the woman she had become when she was with Brandy. The things she had said, they were just pure evil. And what was worse was that she had behaved that way in front of her own daughter. She had always been the jealous type, with a husband as handsome as Aiden it was hard not to be. But she had never been this bad before. Surely she was not threatened by a woman sat on a death row for killing her own husband? In what sick world would Aiden have an affair with such a person? Isla started to cry. If she had even contemplated that Aiden could have had feelings for Brandy, what did that say about the state of their marriage? The person she should really be angry at was herself. Instead she had lashed out at a young girl who was probably already terrified at being so close to her own death. She had acted completely out of character and it was inexcusable. Passion and rage had driven her to this extreme, sat with her daughter in a prison; wondering if she and Brandy were really that different. If under the same circumstances, would she have done the same thing, could she kill? Isla shuddered at the thought.

Aiden lingered at the back of the church as Father West concluded his sermon. He waited patiently as the priest thanked each of his parishioners for coming before approaching him.

'Ah, Mr. Connelly!'

'Father West.'

'How very good to see you! Did you enjoy the service?'

'To be honest I only caught the end of it. I came to see you.'

Father West smiled in surprise.

'To what do I owe the pleasure?'

They wandered back into the pleasant cool of the church and settled down in a front pew.

'Brandy's trial is only a few days away now.'

'Yes, I am aware,' Father West gazed sadly past Aiden.

'Well, I need your help.'

'My help?' his attention quickly returned to the young lawyer.

'I've no doubt that you have heard that I am no longer going to have Brandy tried for murder. I think that she can stand for manslaughter.'

'Which means?'

141

'That her life would at least be spared.'

'That is a brave move, Mr. Connelly.'

'Yeah,' Aiden sighed. 'People around here aren't exactly being supportive. That is why I need you.'

'Me?'

'I need you to go on the stand.'

As a priest, you tread a fine line each and every day between being somebody's confidant and doing what is right. If someone confesses to committing a crime to ease their conscience and make peace with God, you have no right to hand them over to the authorities. You must keep their secret and bear it as your own. There was a time when Brandy White confided in her priest about the terrible struggles she was having to endure in her marriage. Father West did what he thought was right, going to talk things over with Brandon. It had been the wrong decision. He was reluctant to meddle in her affairs again.

'You know what he did to her. Brandy told me that she spoke with you about it, that you tried to reason with Brandon, just before she lost her baby.'

'Perhaps if I had kept my mouth shut that child would be here today,' Father West felt heavy with guilt.

'For all we know he may have beat the kid too. At least now she is free of his abuse.'

'Not really, she has just exchanged one prison for another.'

'If you speak on the stand, a priest, no one will dare question you. You are revered in town. With your testimony the judge will have no choice but to charge Brandy with manslaughter. He may be lenient and give her thirty years, which means that she could be a free woman by the time she is 55, which would give her plenty of life left to live.'

'Yes, but it isn't that easy,' the priest said wearily.

'Why isn't it? All you have to do is stand there and tell the truth!'

'As you said, Mr. Connelly, I am revered in town because I am their connection to God. They look to me as someone that they can trust. If I got up and said what I know about Brandon, their perception of me would change. It may even challenge their faith. As much as I have a duty to Brandy, I also have a duty to Avalon. The truth will hurt so many people.'

'She has no one to fight for her, Father. If you won't stand up for her, who will?'

'You.' Father West placed his hand on Aiden's shoulder.

'You have taken on the entire town in order to try and save her and I admire you greatly for that. But my place is here, in my church, not in a courtroom.'

Aiden shrugged his hand off.

'But she needs you. If she dies over this you will have blood on your hands.'

'How dare you speak to me like that,' Father West shot up, angry.

'You can leave now, Mr. Connelly.'

'Gladly,' Aiden got to his feet and smoothed his shirt down.

'Your loyalty lies with God, not with Avalon or any of the assholes who live here. Your job is to keep people's faith alive; how can you turn your back on her knowing what she has been through?'

'If I don't testify?'

'I have some evidence but it is not nearly enough. Buck Fern will contest every document I produce. I know he will. Brandy has no one who knows her like you do. Only you and I are aware of the atrocities Brandon committed towards her. If you stay silent, how can you come and preach to people about forgiveness and God's will?'

Father West was torn. His feelings for Brandy had already clouded his judgment once before, he would be foolish to let it happen again. But Aiden Connelly was a good, decent man, he could see that. He was willing to sacrifice his reputation, his livelihood, in order to preserve a young woman's life. Surely he was man enough to do the same?

'I'll do it. Just tell me where to be.'

Aiden smiled. He had worried for a moment that the priest would fail him but it looked like he was coming through. With Father West testifying that Brandon had indeed abused his wife

Brandy would surely walk away with a life sentence. The likes of Buck Fern and Clyde White would have to eat their words as they learnt the sordid truth about their beloved Brandon.

'Brandy is lucky to have you on her case. Anyone else would have just let it be.'

'I know.'

'Your wife must be very proud of you.'

Aiden merely nodded, knowing full well that of all the things Isla currently felt towards him, pride was most certainly not one of them.

As Aiden left the church he remembered an old quote; 'If God is on our side, how can we lose?' Indeed, how could he now lose, with Father West on his side? Avalon may well fear the likes of Clyde White and Buck Fern, but surely they feared God even more? He headed over to his offices, jubilant, but knew better than to believe he had won just yet.

In the quiet cool of the office Aiden sat and collected his thoughts. Brandy's trial was fast approaching and he needed to be ready. Knowing that Father West would be testifying helped calm a lot of his nerves. Once the trial was over things could settle down again; he'd take Isla and Meegan out somewhere nice for the day to help make things better. Even though his wife had threatened to leave him if he continued with the manslaughter plea he wasn't backing down. He knew it was just an idle threat from her; she made so many of them that he was used to it by now.

Aiden had been working solidly for an hour when Edmond Copes came bustling through the door, laden down with files.

'Morning, Edmond, are you feeling better?' His partner certainly appeared to be in perfect health as he settled himself down at his desk.

'Ahh, yes, Aiden my man, feeling grand now.' Calling him man, signified that he was not feeling any animosity towards him over the case, which Aiden was extremely thankful for.

Edmond Copes was a kind and warm gentleman whom he would have hated to have lost as a friend over it all.

'Glad to have you back,' he smiled at Edmond fondly.

'It is good to be back. Mrs. Copes just fusses over me all the time when I'm at home. Don't get a minute's peace!'

Edmond spent a few moments arranging the clutter on his desk before pressing down on the intercom button.

'Betty, two coffees,' he said sharply.

'Right away,' came her crackled response.

'Hope the old girl has been alright with you, son. She was just very fond of Brandon and can't take to the revelation that perhaps he, you know…'

'It is OK, I understand. A lot of people have been quite sore about it all.'

'I've no doubt!' Edmond laughed. 'Folks round here can be mighty mean when they want to be.'

'Well,' Aiden hesitated before carrying on. He wanted to confide in someone and felt that he could trust Edmond. He hadn't turned his back on him like everyone else had which said something.

'My wife thinks that Clyde White threatened her and my daughter in the grocery store,' he went with his gut instinct and blurted it out. 'I mean, I've met the guy and he seemed fine. I'm hoping it was just to scare us. He wouldn't ever do anything, would he?'

'What, Clyde?' Edmond's eyes were wide with surprise. 'I'd say no, son, but he is tight with Buck Fern. Those two go way back. I've known him the past, when people have really pissed him off, to have them inundated with speeding fines and parking tickets, small stuff like that. He'd never hurt a soul though.'

'Parking tickets I can handle. She is just pretty spooked.'

'I can imagine. But it will all be over soon and be yesterday's news. You just need to buckle down and ride out the rest of the storm.'

'Yeah, I've just got a feeling that things are going to get a lot worse before they get any better.'

As Betty placed down the coffee mugs she smiled warmly at Edmond but didn't even glance up at Aiden. He didn't like making people mad like this but it had to be done. Edmond chuckled to himself when she left the room.

'She's a stubborn old mule, I'll say that much for her!'

'I hope she doesn't stay stubborn for long though.'

'No, give her a couple of days and, like most women, she will have calmed down and realized she was making a fuss over nothing.'

Aiden wondered how things were going to be after the trial. He knew that everything was riding on the final verdict. If Brandy were to die, people would be happy; if she were allowed to live he was expecting a hefty backlash of anger from Avalon. Either way, he lost.

'How is the case coming along, you all ready?'

'As ready as I'll ever be.'

'It will need to be watertight if you want it to stick.'

'Yeah, I know.'

The evidence that he had gathered was flimsy at best, and Brandy didn't have the best track record for honesty. As long as Father West took to the stand as he had said he would things would be fine.

'You are looking awfully worried,' Edmond noted, concerned.

'I am,' he sighed.

'Just remember not to get your hopes up, or to get too attached. There is every chance that your case might fall through and she will still get the chamber. You need to be ready for that.'

'I am ready,' Aiden lied when really he wasn't ready at all. He was pinning everything on to the hope that Brandy would receive a life sentence. If she were sentenced to death, he didn't know what he would do. He was far too attached, to the case, to her. He knew it wasn't ethical or professional and he hated himself for it, but he cared about Brandy White. Her story was a sad one but he'd give anything for her to at least have something of a happy ending.

The afternoon slipped by and by four Edmond was packing up ready to go home.

'I'll be at the trial.' Aiden was surprised as he hadn't expected him to attend.

'I've being going back and forth on it in my mind as I didn't want to get involved but I figured you might appreciate seeing a friendly face in there.'

'Thanks, Edmond, I will.'

'That doesn't mean that I condone what you are doing. You've upset hell of a lot of people. But you've got moxy, kid, and that I respect. I made the right choice in hiring you.'

'That means a lot.'

'I'd wish you luck, but we both know that it takes a lot more than luck to win a case.'

'It sure does.'

Aiden felt comforted knowing that Edmond would be there. He was ready to defend Brandy; he was ready to take on Avalon.

Chapter Eleven

People in Glass Houses

Time seemed to fly on swift wings and Aiden found himself on the morning of the trial. The grey from the walls of Eastham prison seemed to have leaked out and now coated the rest of the world. A light mist had descended upon Avalon as he drove out to the courthouse. He wondered if many people would show up as it was a fair distance from the town; as he pulled into the parking lot he was surprised by what he saw. There were dozens of people, maybe even a hundred in total. Some had banners bearing messages such as: 'Justice for Brandon.' He recognized the uniform of some Avalon Angels players amongst the faces. It was all quite a commotion. As he got out of his car a woman with a microphone dashed over, followed by a man with a video camera.

'We believe this to be her lawyer,' she was saying to the camera as she ran over. Aiden sighed; this was going to be a long day.

'Hi,' the woman shoved the microphone into his face. 'You are representing Brandy White, who murdered her husband Brandon in cold blood. Is it true that you are no longer conducting this as a murder case?'

He shoved the microphone out of his way and headed towards the courthouse. As people realized who he was they began to gather around him and chant: 'Justice for Avalon's Angel.' Where were the police to calm this mob? He should have known that Buck Fern wouldn't offer any support. He pushed past the protesters and their signs and was glad to get inside the courthouse and away from the madness. He was thankful to be wearing his best suit after he noticed that the cameraman had been tailing him the whole time.

Despite his experience in court, Aiden Connelly was always nervous before a hearing, even if it was a standard divorce proceeding. His nerves had almost cost him his degree. Whilst he passed his exams with flying colours his nerves had been unbearable. He would be sick, shake, and feel faint, all before walking into a courtroom. It was the only time in his life that he ever felt that way. He hadn't even been that nervous on his wedding day! He had no idea why it happened; he had tried everything to calm himself including hypnotherapy. He was in the male restroom splashing his face with cool water as he tried to gather himself. When he looked at his reflection, the man in the mirror seemed strong and poised even though inside he felt as if all his organs had turned to jelly. He needed to be strong for Brandy. He looked the part even though he didn't feel it. He wished he hadn't given up smoking; he could really use a cigarette. Smoking was yet another thing he did that Isla hated and during their marriage she had slowly drummed the habit out of him with her persistent nagging. He knew it was in his best interest to stop smoking; he just would have been happier to have quit when he was ready rather than being forced into it. He ran his hands through his hair, took one last deep breath and pushed open the toilet door, full of determination.

Brandy White had never been in a courtroom before so she had no idea what to expect. She was thankful to be out of the prison and for the change of scenery. The guards had ushered her in through a back entrance after noticing the gathering crowd of protesters out front. She was still wearing the regulation garish orange jumpsuit with her hands cuffed together. She had hoped that they might allow her to wear something smarter, perhaps put some make-up on. Although Brandy had lost her crown, the beauty queen mentality remained and when she knew she would be facing a room full of people she immediately wanted to look her best. She had tried to fix her hair as best she could with her very limited resources but felt disappointed with the results. She looked drab and washed out. As a woman, her mascara, blush, and lipstick were all part of a mask which she would paint on. It gave her confidence and something to hide behind. If you looked lovely it helped some way to making you feel lovely too. But Brandy was feeling awful. She sat in a small room, waiting for Aiden Connelly to come and speak with her before they went out to face the angry faces of Avalon. This time there would be no glass between them. She would be able to smell his cologne, the coffee on his breath.

'Morning, Brandy,' he came in and sat down. He looked so handsome in his suit although he was a little pale and seemed agitated.

'Good morning, Mr. Connelly, I'm so glad to see you.' He smiled at her and she felt her anxieties beginning to slip away.

'Now, what is going to happen is you'll take to the stand and I'll ask you a few questions and so will the opposing lawyer. You must answer everything completely honestly, no matter how awful, OK?'

'Yes, OK.'

'Other people will also take the stand. They might say cruel things about you; you need to be ready to hear that.'

'I'll be fine, Mr. Connelly. I've heard it all before.'

'Just, try not to get too upset, I know it's hard. Remember that I'm there and that I believe in you,' before he knew what he was doing he reached out and touched her hand. There was no glass to stop him. Her skin was soft and smooth, like rose petals. His touch felt warm and made Brandy tingle all over. She hadn't been touched by a man for a long time, not like this, delicately. She was used to fists and punches, not palms and gentleness.

Despite himself, Aiden's hand remained there for a moment. It felt good to finally be able to connect to Brandy, but touching her, feeling her flesh, made his heart ache. He had to save her; he had to make people see what he saw. He gave her hand a gentle squeeze as he got up to leave.

'I'll see you in the courtroom; it will all be fine.'

'I trust you, Mr. Connelly.'

She kept that moment with her, when his hand touched hers, as she was led into the courtroom and row after row of accusing, hate-filled eyes bore down upon her. Brandy bowed her head, not in shame but in fear. She could hear their cruel whispers and angry taunts but she ignored them. All that mattered was Aiden and now that she was sat beside him, facing the judge, she at last felt safe. He was going to save her, she just knew it.

First to take the stand was the old dinosaur himself, Buck Fern. He highlighted his long history with the town of Avalon, how he lived only to serve the people. He told the jury how he had nothing but fond memories of Brandon White.

'He was a good kid, no doubt about that,' he told them.

'I never had to have a cross word with him. He was one of a kind.' Aiden felt sick hearing the old man being such a sycophant.

'You all knew Brandon, probably for many years,' he called out to the courtroom, brainwashing them.

'He would never hurt a soul.' People in the room were sobbing into handkerchiefs, comforting one another; it was absurd. True to his word, Edmond was there looking solemn. Some of the Avalon Angels were inside, probably brought in to testify; also Aiden spotted some men in lumberjack shirts who he assumed to be Avalon Pine workers who would no doubt sing the praises of their deceased co-worker. If it were a popularity contest, Brandon White would win hands down.

'She's always been a liar,' as expected Buck Fern had begun a character assassination on Brandy. 'I'll never forget when she lied about having her high school diploma. She let the whole town down,' his eyes, no wiser through age, gave Brandy a disdainful glance. Aiden could see that she was struggling to hold back tears.

'They are just words, Brandy,' he whispered softly to her. They were just words, but Buck Fern was an influential man and his words could do a lot of damage.

'You say you never had a cross word with Mr. White?' It was now Aiden's turn to cross-examine the witness and he wasn't going to hold anything back.

'That's true.'

'What about the times he was drunk and disorderly or caught driving under the influence. I've read the files, you were the arresting officer. Did you not chastise him them?'

Buck Fern laughed a jolly, carefree laugh, the kind a man in a Santa Claus suit might force out to delight young children.

'Boys will be boys, Mr. Connelly. We all get a little too drunk sometimes and do stupid things.'

'Like hitting your wife?'

'No! Like being a bit too rowdy with the boys. Brandon wasn't violent!'

'He wasn't violent, yet he was an extremely competent football player. A game, if I'm not mistaken, which relies on a certain degree of violence from the players?'

'Yes, but that's just a game!' The crotchety old sheriff was getting annoyed.

'Did Brandon enjoy a drink?'

'Yes, I think so.'

'Did he drink often?'

'Not to my knowledge.'

'When he did drink, did he drink a lot?'

'Define a lot, Mr. Connelly.'

'Was he over the limit?'

'Sometimes.'

'Is it possible that under the influence of alcohol he had the potential to become a violent man?'

'No, it is not possible.'

'You know that for a fact?'

'Yes.'

'You spied on him did you; did you watch him at all times? When he was in the shower, when he was making love to his wife?'

'No! Don't be ridiculous!'

'So, how do you know what went on in the privacy of his own home?'

Aiden was pleased with how the trial was progressing. When he presented his evidence to the court he was satisfied that he managed to get his point across. He made a point of focusing on how Buck Fern was always first on the scene. The old man tried to pass it off as him just being in the area so responding first, but Aiden felt that he had, successfully, raised the suspicion that the sheriff was covering for Brandon.

'She did it to herself,' Buck said with fake emotion when Aiden quizzed him over the night of the shattered vase.

'It was obvious; Brandon said she did it all the time.'

'If it was so obvious, why didn't you send her for a psychological evaluation?'

'Brandon didn't want it.'

'Shouldn't you have overruled him, for Brandy's sake?'

'It's a husband's duty to take care of his wife. I respected his decision.'

'Did you respect him when he beat her? Was that taking care of his wife?'

'She did it to herself,' Buck Fern remained composed. No doubt he was a pro at court appearances and knew just how to manipulate the court. However, Aiden was done with old man and relatively happy with how things had gone. The judge called for the next witness, Clyde White.

Clyde White looked haggard, as if he hadn't slept in days. His eyes were bloodshot and sunken. He was clearly a man consumed with grief. As he took to the stand he wiped a phantom tear from his eye. Aiden recalled how Clyde had seemed when he had gone to visit him at Avalon Pines; whilst filled with a deep sorrow he had been together. The man before him now was a wreck. Either it was all for show or the stress of the trial was getting to him.

Like Buck Fern before him, Clyde was quick to highlight what a key member of the community he was, how his business employed almost half of Avalon's workers. He recalled, tearily, what a wonderful child Brandon had been and how he had grown into an amazing young man. He focused heavily on the pride he felt when his son had won the state championship with his high school football team. Aiden knew that the history lesson was unnecessary; it was merely a tactic to curry favor with the jury. It was wasting precious time yet the judge let it go when

Aiden contested. Finally, it was his time to question Clyde White.

'Mr. White, were you close to Brandy when she was married to your son?'

'Not at all,' the businessman snapped.

'Were you ever close to her? Were you ever fond of her?'

'No, I could tell that she was trouble, and now, my poor son...' Clyde produced a handkerchief and dabbed at his eyes.

'Keep it together, please, Mr. White.' He wanted to add that this was not a drama class but didn't want to turn the jury against him by appearing insensitive.

'Did you, or did you not give Brandy away on her wedding day?'

'Yes, I did, but I don't see what that has to do with anything!'

'I'd say that giving somebody away on their wedding day is a pretty big deal, and only something you'd do if you were extremely fond of them.'

'She had nobody else. I did it out of pity.'

'How big of you. So you were never a father figure to her?'

'Never.'

'Yet you played a big part in Brandon's life?'

'Yes, of course, what are you implying?' Clyde White was starting to get annoyed and the fragile father persona was beginning to slip away.

'I'd say, in my opinion, a good father embraces their son's chosen spouse, treats them as a daughter. Yet you openly admit that you were never kind to Brandy, even though Brandon loved her. That doesn't sound like a good father to me.'

'This has nothing to do with why she killed my son!' he slammed his fist against the dark wood of the stand as real tears of frustration pricked his eyes.

'Maybe it has everything to do with it,' Aiden taunted. 'You didn't know Brandon well enough to understand why he loved Brandy and had made her his wife. If you failed to understand a choice this monumental in your son's life, what else about him didn't you know? It seems to me that he was basically a stranger to you, so how can you swear that he never struck his young wife?'

'He wouldn't do that, I know my boy.'

'Actually, you've made it clear that you didn't know him that well at all.'

Clyde White was seething. He was being made to look a fool at his dead son's trial. Aiden Connelly was cocky but also cunning, which made for a most infuriating combination.

'Would Brandy visit your home much, at Christmases, birthdays?'

'Yes.'

'What about any other times? She lived in the same town, it would make sense if you saw her on a weekly basis. Yet you didn't.'

'She only came over on holidays.'

'Why was that?'

'We didn't like her, she didn't care for our company much, it was mutual.'

'Mrs. White claims to have seen you as a father figure, sounds like she liked you an awful lot.'

Clyde White looked over at Brandy; her head was down so that he couldn't see her eyes, only her halo of golden hair.

'Do you think that maybe she didn't come around as she was covered in cuts and bruises that Brandon didn't want you to see?'

'No, I don't think that.'

'Because Brandy knew no one in town. The Whites were her only family so it shocks me that you saw so little of her. Unless she was hiding something. Did you ever see marks on her?'

The businessman was silent.

'Remember you are under oath, Mr. White. Did you ever see any marks on Brandy White?'

'Occasionally, she had a black eye or a cut lip, maybe. But she was a clumsy oaf of a girl.'

'So, on the very few occasions that you did see your daughter-in-law she displayed marks which could have been

155

inflicted upon her by violent means? This clearly indicates that Mrs. White was, more often than not, bruised and battered. And as for your reasoning that these wounds were the outcome of clumsy behavior..?' Aiden motioned over to Brandy '… she has the delicate frame of a ballerina, far from that of a clumsy oaf. I find it hard to believe that someone as dainty as she would be regularly losing her footing.'

The trial was going well, really well. He had successfully navigated his way past the two heavyweights that were Buck Fern and Clyde White. Now all that was left was for Father West to deliver his testimony and they would be on the home straight. Court was adjourned for a much needed break so Aiden went to seek out the priest.

Aiden scanned the corridors as he wandered off to get a coffee. People were getting drinks, discussing how the trial was progressing; all of them gave him scowling glares as he walked past. He knew all along it was going to be tough, so he took their anger in his stride.

'You are doing well, my boy!' Edmond slapped Aiden on the back as he was pouring himself a drink.

'Thank you, Edmond.' He noticed that his colleague was looking about nervously, probably because he didn't want anyone seeing him offering the young lawyer any encouragement. His reputation was still intact and he wanted to keep it that way.

'Buck and Clyde are tough nuts to crack.'

'They sure are.'

'Still, you'll need an ace up your sleeve to round this all up.'

'Yeah.'

'Here,' Edmond pulled a silver hip flask from beneath his jacket and tipped a little of the contents into Aiden's coffee mug.

'Just to give you some extra pep in your step!' he winked.

'I can't drink while I'm working!' Aiden was shocked.

'Nonsense, we all do it. Its fine, only a little sip, it's nothing. It will help calm the nerves,' he slapped Aiden on the back once more before sauntering off back to the courtroom.

From the swagger in his step it seemed he had enjoyed more than a little sip that morning. When he was gone from view, Aiden tipped his coffee into a nearby plant pot.

'Court is now in session!' the presiding judge declared. Aiden stood up, ready to retrieve the ace from up his sleeve. He hadn't yet seen Father West but that didn't bother him. The priest had told him he'd show and the word from a man of God was as strong as oak. He wasn't worried.

'I'd like to call to the stand Father Patrick West'. Gasps and whispers swept through the assortment of characters present as they received the scandalous news that a priest would be testifying, against the accused killer no less! Then the whispers died down and a silence settled over the room. Aiden looked out at the sea of faces, most of which were vaguely familiar, but none were that of Father West. Now, he began to feel nervous.

'Where is your witness?' the judge asked, clearly annoyed.

'He will be here.'

People were getting restless and beginning to snigger. Where the hell was he? Five minutes passed and still no priest.

'Mr. Connelly, approach the bench,' the judge ordered.

'Where is your witness?' he lowered his voice so that only Aiden could hear, even though the crowd leant forward and strained to listen.

'He said he'd be here. If I could just go and call him; he must have been detained.'

'Is this a stalling tactic?'

'No, no, I swear.'

'You have five minutes and not a second more.'

Aiden dashed out of the courtroom, cell phone in hand, and frantically dialed the number for Father West's church. Six rings, seven rings.

'Pick up, pick up,' he muttered angrily.

Ten rings, eleven rings.

'Dammit!' he punched his fist against the wall in frustration.

'Something wrong?' the concerned voice belonged to Edmond.

'Looks like I just lost my ace,' Aiden leant against the wall and slumped to the ground.

'You were going to put Father West on the stand?'

'He knew everything. He even tried to reason with Brandon to stop him hurting Brandy anymore. He told me he'd be here.'

'Coming here and testifying against Brandon White, he had a lot to lose, son. Don't surprise me he didn't show.'

'What do I do now?'

Edmond saw fear in the young man's eyes.

'Have you called him?'

'Yeah, no answer.'

'Do you think that you can stall for any longer?'

'Not really, why?'

Edmond Copes was already dashing off down the corridor.

'Just stall!' He yelled. 'I'll call as soon as I have news.'

It went against Aiden's principals but he lied, he said he had a family emergency that he had to quickly attend to. The judge saw right through it but granted him an extended break all the same. He had thirty minutes to find Father West. He continued calling the church but to no avail. All his hopes were pinned on Edmond.

'Stalling, are we?' Buck Fern cornered Aiden in the corridor, a sly grin spread across his old face.

'Just have some things that I have to attend to.'

'You are just delaying the inevitable.'

'How do you sleep at night?' Aiden spat, too stressed and anxious to play games with the sheriff.

'Like a baby,' he laughed. Aiden pushed past him and dialed the church again. Ring after ring, but no answer. Time was running out.

Suddenly his cell phone sprung to life in his hands, alerting him to an incoming call.

'Hello?'

'Mr. Connelly?' It was Father West!

'Where the hell are you?' Aiden ducked into the men's restroom to get some privacy.

158

'I'm sorry.'

'When are you getting here? We don't have much time!'

'I'm not.'

'Wh…what do you mean you're not!' he was furious.

'I can't do it, I'm sorry.' The line went dead.

'She's going to die you prick, how can you do this!' he yelled into his handset before throwing it across the floor. He leant against a sink and let his head fall into his hands.

'Aiden,' Edmond came into the toilet, breathless.

'I'm sorry, son, there is a right crowd outside, I couldn't even get out of the parking lot, and I've been trying for twenty minutes. I had to just give up in the end.'

'It's OK, he just called.'

'And?'

'He's not coming.'

'Shit.'

'I think I'll take that drink now.'

The trial resumed, minus Father West. Aiden tried not to let Brandy see how defeated he felt. Perhaps the evidence he had accumulated would be enough? He lived in hope. He delivered his closing statement to the jury and begged them to be humane to Brandy.

'Brandy White is more than a victim of circumstance. She was routinely bullied, beaten and broken down by a man who had vowed to love and protect her. She had no choice but to take his life as she was acting in self-defense. If she had not killed him, he would have killed her, there is no doubt about that. Spare her life, do not let him win.'

He rarely ever spoke to God; he was unsure if he even existed, but he offered up a prayer all the same.

'Don't let her die,' it seemed a reasonable enough request.

The twenty minutes that the jury took to deliberate their verdict felt like twenty days. Aiden paced the corridor relentlessly. Around him, people whispered and prophesied on what the outcome may be. They all wanted the same thing: Brandy's blood.

'Whatever the verdict, you are detached, remember?' Edmond placed a hand upon Aiden's shoulder as he spoke quietly into his ear.

'Yeah, of course.' But he wasn't detached, far from it. He was involved.

As he sat back down beside Brandy, facing the judge, his heart was pounding so loudly he was sure that the entire room were being deafened by it. A persistent drum that was gaining in speed, like a war cry. His palms were sweaty and his leg was twitching uncontrollably. The last time he had felt this tense was when Isla had sat on the toilet, peed on to a stick and that they then had had to sit and watch for two minutes. He hadn't liked the outcome then, but ultimately it had made him happy. Brandy's life being spared would make him happy; it would restore his faith in humanity. Just like in the Disney movies that his daughter was so terribly fond of; someone wishes upon a star and something amazing can happen. Maybe, here, today, something amazing was going to happen. Justice would surely be served.

'We have reached our verdict,' a slip of white paper was passed to the judge. He read the writing upon it with an expressionless face. With a flat tone he delivered the jury's decision.

'The court finds Brandy White guilty of first degree murder.'

In the courtroom people rose to their feet, applauding, as Aiden felt the world around him slipping away. He leant against the table to steady himself, breathing deeply, trying to remain calm and composed. Brandy's eyes were wide with fear and sadness. People were whooping and cheering, embracing one another, so delighted at the revelation that a life was to end. Their reaction was more devastating than the news that she was to die. It was more than she could bear. Tears flowed down her cheeks and her body shook.

'They hate me,' she whispered to Aiden.

'I don't hate you.'

'Stand for sentencing,' the judge ordered as the crowd settled down. Aiden felt sick and disillusioned. How could this have happened?

'Brandy White, I hereby sentence you to death via the gas chamber.' Brandy collapsed sobbing into Aiden's arms. He held her for as long as he could but the guards were trying to lead her away.

'I'll do something, Brandy, don't worry. This isn't final,' he said, chasing after her. But it was final; he had no cards left to play. He felt defeated.

'I'm sorry, son, it's the way it goes sometimes,' Edmond placed a caring arm around Aiden's shoulders.

'There is no one to blame.'

'But there is,' Aiden thought. Father West was to blame. He may as well have signed her death warrant himself. His sadness began to turn into rage. He was going to make the priest pay.

Chapter Twelve

Let God Be the Judge

Aiden looked down at his French toast which he had barely touched. He had no appetite. He had barely eaten for days, not since Brandy was sentenced. He spent his days appealing her case relentlessly but to no avail. And now today was upon him, when her sentence was due to be carried out. Today, Brandy White was to enter the gas chamber and wouldn't come out alive. His heart was breaking whilst the rest of Avalon were jubilant. Brandon White was still their golden boy; Brandy still the vile villain who had taken him away from them. It was all so wrong.

'I've got to go,' he told Isla quietly. They were barely speaking at the moment. She sensed that she needed to tread carefully around her husband because he was wallowing in sadness, so she was giving him his space. A part of her resented his melancholy; she felt jealous of how deeply Brandy had affected him which she knew was foolish. Aiden was just a passionate, caring man.

'You haven't touched your breakfast,' she said softly as he put on his jacket.

'I'm not hungry.'

'But you've got to eat.'

'I don't feel like it!' he snapped. He was exhausted through lack of sleep and his stomach refused to stop doing somersaults. He reminded himself that it would all be over soon; the anger from the people of Avalon towards him was already beginning to subside. The general consensus was that he had been manipulated by the vixen that is Brandy, bewitched by her beauty. Isla overheard their theories in the store, on the street, but she ignored them. Once Brandy was gone she would get her husband back and that was all she cared about.

Even Meegan sensed the atmosphere in the house as she was being uncharacteristically quiet around her father. Whenever she did giggle or clap he just watched her with sad, dead eyes so she would stop. The little girl reasoned that if she wasn't making her Daddy happy anymore, she might as well just stop. Isla hated seeing her family like this, over the impending death of somebody who meant nothing to them, was basically a stranger, but she didn't speak up for fear of turning Aiden against her. He was so fragile about it all.

'So, today's the day,' she tried to coax some conversation out of him. Something, anything was better than the silence which was becoming the void that was their marriage.

'Today's the day,' he echoed flatly.

'It is for the best,' she rubbed her hand across his back; he was cold to the touch.

'Is it?' he looked at his wife with empty eyes. Although she had not seen him cry he appeared to have no tears left; he was like a shell.

'Aid, it will all be over soon and things can return to normal.'

'You smashed my mug.'

'What?' she was taken completely by surprise by his random mention of the shattered mug.

'My mug was normal. You destroyed that.'

Isla tried not to read too much into what her husband was saying; he was sleep deprived and talking nonsense.

'Do you want me to drive you? You look exhausted.'

'No, I'll be fine,' he declined her offer.

She kissed him on the cheek but he didn't appear to notice. With feet like lead, Aiden dragged himself to his car and drove off towards Eastham Ladies Penitentiary to watch a light be extinguished.

The prison was a hive of activity. Likes ants, people were scurrying back and forth, up and down corridors doing their various chores. The parking lot was bursting at the seams as Avalon residents flocked to see the execution of Brandy White. There was a heavy media presence; numerous reporters were already broadcasting from outside, it was big news.

The sun was refusing to shine that day which added to Aiden's somber mood. He pushed past the morbid spectators, disgusted by their vulgarity and lack of humanity. They were behaving as if they were at a football game. Their attitude sickened him to his very core. He kept his head down and navigated his way into the prison. None of these people had ever bothered about Brandy before, but now that their blood lust had taken over, here they were.

'Brandy White, local disgraced beauty queen will today be executed for the brutal murder of her husband, Brandon White,' he caught the beginning of one reporter's broadcast just as the doors slammed shut behind him. The grey of the walls felt like it was seeping into his skin, crawling through his veins and turning his entire universe into a dull, lackluster shade of charcoal. He walked the familiar route to Brandy in a trance, as though he were a zombie. In a way, he felt like the undead. A part of him had truly died when Brandy was sentenced to death. The part that lives in all of us which believes that there is some good in the world, like when you drop all your shopping bags and a stranger stops to help you pick them up. No dark motive, just someone being a 'Good' Samaritan, helping for helping's sake, that part in him, which we call hope, was gone. Aiden no longer lived in a world were justice prevailed and you could rely on the kindness of strangers. Goodness was gone, replaced with cruelty and the sad realization that some wicked people were indifferent to life and death.

A lump grew in his throat as he grew ever closer to the room with the familiar Perspex wall. What was he going to say to her? How was your last meal? It was absurd. There was nothing he could possibly say to make her feel better, or himself for that matter. He had failed Brandy and he felt ashamed to even face her. But he knew he had to comfort her; he owed her that much. But it was going to be so very hard, to see her, and to know that it would be the last time.

He was so consumed with his emotions that he failed to notice that he was being guided on a new, unfamiliar route.

'Where are we going?' he asked, his senses snapping back.

'To a private room, Mr. Connelly. Mrs. White requested to see you alone; it was her last request.'

He felt his pulse quicken. She wanted to see him alone? Would there be a glass wall separating them? He thought about everything they had said to one another, and everything that had been left unsaid. It stuck in his mind how fearful she was of everyone hating her.

'The people outside.'

'What about them?' The prison guard guiding him stopped and turned to face him. Her face was stern but there was a warmth to her which hinted that perhaps, beyond these grey walls she was a happy, jovial woman. She stood a good three inches taller than Aiden and was well fed. He felt slightly intimidated.

'They won't be present at the...' he couldn't bring himself to say it out loud.

'At the execution?' she finished his sentence for him.

'Yes, I don't want them in there. It will devastate Brandy to see them all in there, looking at...'

'I understand but you don't need to worry. Only yourself and close friends and family of the victim are granted access into the viewing chamber. She need never know about the circus outside.'

'Well, that's good then.'

The guard turned to continue but then stopped herself and faced Aiden again.

'I know what them people out there are saying, Mr. Connelly. I live in Meadowgate, the next town over from Avalon and news spreads like crabs at a college party. But I don't think Brandy is a monster, far from it. I've seen the marks on her, I know you're not lying. She's a good person and I'll miss her around here. But God, he knows the truth, he won't judge, he'll welcome an angel like that with open arms. I just thought you should know, because you seem different from the others. Like you have a heart.'

'Thank you.'

'Just, don't let her think everybody hates her, because it isn't like that. It is more than my jobs worth to say that to her mind, but perhaps you can. You seem like a good man. Don't let all this change you.'

Aiden thanked her again and they continued their journey towards Prisoner 929. He felt strangely comforted by the random insightfulness shown by the guard.

'The people of Avalon have congregated here to see justice served. I have with me the victim's father, Clyde White,' the reporter told the camera.

'Mr. White, how are you feeling at this traumatic time? Will today give you closure?' She shoved the microphone towards Clyde. Gone was the emotional wreck of a man who had appeared in court. In his place stood an immaculate, well turned out gentleman in a suit who looked every inch the successful businessman. The only traces of the sadness eating away at his heart were the lines etched around his eyes and across his forehead. He had aged ten years in the past few months.

'I have come to see my son's killer get what she deserves, but it won't bring my son back. My family and I will be forever lost without him.'

Isla switched the television off. Even on screen, with the backdrop of the prison, Clyde White still made her feel uncomfortable. She carried on braiding Meegan's hair, who was sat quietly on her lap, playing with one of her dolls.

'Will Daddy be home soon?' she asked hopefully.

'Yes, Daddy will be home very soon, baby.' She tried to sound upbeat for her daughter but knew she wasn't very convincing.

'Is Daddy going to be OK?'

'Yes, he is going to be fine,' of that she was certain. Aiden was a strong man; he would bounce back from all of this, he had to.

Brandy White was afraid. Despite all her religious beliefs, she had no real idea of what was waiting for her in the great beyond. Perhaps heaven did exist, but in that case, hell must exist too and what if she were destined for there? An afterlife spent in fiery torment. She shivered at the thought. Or perhaps, after you took your last breath, nothing happens. The world just stops, for you at least, as your mortal life comes to an end. Maybe all that awaited her was never-ending darkness. Wherever she was going, she would rather stay where she was. Even though her life had been far from ideal she wasn't ready to say goodbye to it. Brandon had been a monster; there was no doubt about that. But now, in her final moments, she found herself wondering if he had really deserved to die.

When Aiden entered the room he had to fight back the tears which immediately formed in his eyes. Prisoner 929 was sat, hands in lap, with a wistful look upon her face. She looked more beautiful than ever, heavenly even. The guard closed the door behind Aiden and, for the first time ever, they were completely alone.

There was no Perspex glass wall in place forming a barrier between them, no silver bracelets around Brandy's tiny wrists to restrict her movement. There were just two plastic chairs and a wooden table. She was still wearing the garish orange jumpsuit but she did not look like a criminal to Aiden; she looked like a victim.

'I'm so sorry,' he blurted, as without thinking he sat down and grabbed her hands across the table. She was deathly cold.
'Don't be sorry,' her voice so soft, so sweet. 'You did your best.' She smiled at him and his heart melted.
'Father West, he was supposed to testify, but he didn't show. If he'd just spoken about what he knew,' he tightened his grip on her hands in anger.

167

'Father West?' she asked, alarmed.

'Yes, he was willing to take the stand for you. Well, he said he was, he obviously lied.'

'A priest would never testify in court, Mr. Connelly, it just isn't right. Don't be angry with him.'

Brandy White amazed him so. All her life people had mistreated her, been unkind, yet there wasn't a malicious bone in her body. She was so gracious, so loving, so sweet.

'What will happen?' her voice had suddenly gone very quiet, almost inaudible.

'What will happen to me in the gas chamber?'

Aiden didn't want to answer her. What happened to criminals in the gas chamber was horrific. He detested it. Capital punishment had its benefits, but the chamber was just inhumane; it was how you would exterminate a rat, not a human life. He had seen people taken to the chair, injected and brought to the chamber numerous times. It was always horrific and unpleasant to watch somebody die no matter what they had done to deserve it. The chamber, however, was truly the cruelest way to go. In many states it was no longer used; sadly that was not the case here. The last time he had witnessed it in use was when he had sent down a convicted pedophile that had ritualistically drugged, raped and killed a dozen six-year-old little girls over the course of a decade. But as Aiden watched the man drop down to the ground, clawing at his throat as the deadly fumes invaded his body, he felt pity for him. That man was a monster, a vile creature who knew no shame, no love, nothing. Yet he didn't deserve to die like that, with people watching, cheering. It was awful. And now, knowing that Brandy was about to receive that same fate, he felt sick.

'It will be over so quickly you won't feel a thing.' He was lying. It was all a spectacular for the disturbed audience watching. The loved ones of the victim who wanted to see the condemned suffer. The pedophile had coughed up liters of blood before shaking violently, and then ceasing to move. Brandy already had terror in her eyes; he didn't want to make that worse. He couldn't bear to upset her anymore. He already felt that he had failed her. Now, if he were to make her cry, it would be more than he could handle.

'I know that God will welcome me into His kingdom, He will understand why I did what I did,' Brandy was trying to convince herself as much as she was Aiden.

'You are so brave; you are by far the bravest person I have ever known.'

'You've got to keep fighting for people, Mr. Connelly. You are a good man and I know that you are going to help so many people.'

'Yes, but I wanted to help you,' he was on the verge of crying.

'You did help me, Mr. Connelly.'

'Please, Brandy, call me Aiden.'

'OK, Aiden. You did help me, more than you realize. You showed me that the world isn't completely full of hate, that some people can care.' She gazed at him with adoring eyes.

'You are truly an angel.' She blushed at this.

'Well, Aiden, God knows that even angels fall. I just wish I had been given my chance to shine, to show the world what I can be. My Ma, she said to me once, 'Baby girl, this world won't give you all that you desire because we come from a humble place, but that don't mean that you're not a star. Because not all stars sparkle, just because you can't see them, because they are too far away, that don't mean that they're not there.' I think that was her way of telling me that she thought I was a star.'

'You are a star.'

'I wish she was here today. Just because everyone in that room is there because they hate me. If my Ma were there, at least there would be one person who loved me.'

A solitary tear danced down her soft cheek.

'I love you,' as Aiden said the words he realized that he did love her, that he had loved her all along. Brandy represented everything good in the world; she was beautiful, kind, humble and patient. He had never met anyone like her before.

'You love me?' now she was crying, her vision obscured by her tears.

'Yes, more than anything.'

'I love you too,' she sobbed.

Aiden rose to his feet and went round to embrace Brandy. She felt so small in his arms, so fragile. He wanted to hold her there forever, to protect her, to save her.

'How am I going to live without you?' he said into her hair. He inhaled her intoxicating smell of vanilla, oranges and peach. She smelt like heaven. His senses were on fire, trying to take in every last detail of it and burn it forever into his memory.

Brandy pulled back from the embrace and gazed up at him.

'Thank you for believing in me.'

Aiden leant down and placed his lips on hers. It was electrifying. She kissed him back and he had never felt more alive. His heart was racing.

A sharp knock at the door bought them both back to reality. It was time.

Aiden watched Brandy being led away, knowing that he was only moments from losing her forever. She looked back at him mournfully but there was a resilience in her step that told him that she had accepted her tragic fate and was going to face her maker with her head held high.

'Oh, Mr. Connelly, thank God,' came a breathless voice from behind.

Turning, Aiden was shocked to see Father West. The priest's face was flushed and his hair disheveled as if he had been running. He was clearly panicked about something.

'If you have come to read Brandy her last rights you are too late,' Aiden could not conceal the disgust in his voice. 'I don't know how you can even have the audacity to show up.' He turned away from Father West, having nothing else to say, at least not here. Another time, another place, preferably when he had a good few beers in him, he would have gladly punched him square in the face, man of God or not.

'Please, it is imperative that I talk with you.'

'Sorry, Father, but I'm all talked out,' Aiden began to walk off, he was already distressed enough about losing Brandy; he didn't need any more aggravation.

'Mr. Connelly, I must insist, it is urgent,' he grabbed at the young lawyer's sleeve, preventing him for walking away.

'Urgent, is it, Father? Really? Like you even understand the meaning of the word! Get off me, I've somewhere to be, no thanks to you, you disgust me.' He shrugged him off and carried on walking but the priest followed.

'What I have to say to you, I'm afraid that it is a matter of life and death.'

'Oh really?' Aiden yelled dramatically. 'Brandy is going to die because of *you*. You were too cowardly to testify for her and in a few minutes she will be dead. I hope you are happy to let that sit on your conscience for the rest of your life. Maybe if you pray real hard God will forgive you, but I never will.'

'I couldn't take to the stand; I know I let you and Brandy down, that is why I'm here.'

'Why couldn't you take the stand? Were you too worried about the precious people of Avalon hating you? You were willing to sacrifice a life for your own reputation!'

'That isn't it!'

'Then what the hell is it?'

'I couldn't testify because I cannot lie.'

'What?'

'Please, there is much I need to tell you. We haven't got much time.'

Aiden found himself once again in the informal interview room, only this time he was sitting across from Father West instead of Brandy. The priest was clearly shaken by something; he was sweating profusely and his eyes were constantly darting around the room in a nervous manner.

'Don't waste my time; say what you need to say.'

Patrick West took a moment to collect himself. His entire world was about to change but he had no choice.

'When you went to see Brandy, after I spoke with you, I told you to tell her to tell you everything, but you didn't, did you?' His voice was calmer now.

Thinking back on the times he had spoken with Brandy Aiden tried to recall what he had, and had not, said to her.

'No, I don't think I did. Why, what does it matter?'

Father West looked at Aiden with a strange desperation in his eyes, like an animal being led to the slaughter.

'It matters because the poor girl has been harboring a secret, a secret which she was willing to die for.'

'What secret?'

'She didn't kill Brandon White.'

'Then who did?'

'I did.'

Silence settled between them as Aiden absorbed the huge bombshell which had just been dropped on him. It didn't make sense.

'Brandy told me herself that she killed him, how she did it.'

'She is lying.'

'Or maybe you are lying in some ill-judged attempt to clear your conscience for letting her down.'

'No.'

'If it's true, why didn't you speak up sooner?'

'I was afraid.'

'And now?' Aiden snapped, still struggling to believe what he was hearing.

'I cannot let an innocent woman die. The truth needs to be told.'

'OK then, tell me the truth.'

Patrick West thought back to that fateful night when his plan to help Brandy White escape her abusive husband had tragically backfired.

'After she came to church, pregnant and beat up, I decided to talk to Brandon. I thought it was the best thing to do at the time. He had always been a polite enough young man, he seemed approachable. I had hoped that I could make him see sense, help steer him back onto the right path. But I was wrong. He put on an act for me, apologizing over and over, even crying, that he was going to repent his awful ways and treat Brandy like a queen. Like a fool I believed him. Not long after she was back

172

in hospital because of him and she had lost her baby. I knew that I was to blame. If I hadn't interfered...'

The priest shook his head sadly at what might have been.

'When she was discharged from hospital, I went round to see her. He had messed her up pretty bad and she was clearly terrified. I had to help her get out of there. Over the next couple of months I helped her save up a bit of money and found a suitable safe house a few states over. She could start a new life from there, finally be free of him. She told me he was going away one weekend and it seemed like the perfect time for her to make her move. She packed her bags and was all ready to leave. I went round to collect her as I was going to drop her off at the station and when I walked in Brandon had her pinned on the floor, his arms around her neck, he was killing her.'

'So you attacked him?'

'Not straight away. At first I tried to pull him off but he was so strong, much stronger than me. I was yelling at him, begging him to release her, but he wasn't listening and her face was starting to turn blue. I had no choice.'

He dropped his head in his hands in shame.

'I picked up a knife and launched myself at him; I lost myself in an angry frenzy. How could he treat good, sweet Brandy like that? She had never hurt anybody. I resented him, loathed him and wanted to make him pay. I didn't mean to kill him. I just wanted to hurt him but I got carried away. I stopped when Brandy began to scream. She was horrified. She looked at me like I was a monster.'

'Then what happened?'

'I calmed her down and we talked it through. I told her that I had only been doing God's will, and then, Lord forgive me, I told her that she had to take the blame. I couldn't go to jail for murder; I'm a priest, people look to me as their moral centre. It would destroy Avalon if word ever got out. Brandy is so devoted to her faith, and therefore me, that she agreed. I told her she would probably have to die and she was willing even to do that. I made it clear that no one was to know the truth. She waited until I was long gone before alerting the authorities, and you know the rest.'

Aiden couldn't quite believe his ears. It was a lot of information to take in.

'So Brandy is innocent?'

'Completely.'

'You were going to let her die for this,' he began to grow angry.

'No, I couldn't, that is why I came to see you. I know I should have told you sooner, but, this will destroy everything.'

'No, it will destroy you.'

'I never meant to kill him. I just wanted to save her.'

'Well, now is your chance to save her, by telling everyone the truth.'

'So what happens now?'

'I get to go be the hero and save the damsel in distress.' Aiden's hand was on the door handle when he turned back to Father West.

'Just in case you are still not as good as your word, I taped our entire conversation.'

Time was running out as Aiden ran down corridors, dashing past confused guards. Brandy White was innocent, he wanted to cry out at the top of his lungs. Now, he could truly save her.

Aiden had never moved so fast before in his adult life. He nearly slipped on the slick flooring a number of times but he didn't dare slow down. He was almost at the viewing room when he crashed straight into the back of Clyde White.

'Easy, where's the fire?' he smoothed down his suit and shot Aiden an annoyed glare.

'I need to talk to the-'

'Whoa, whoa, you can't go running around like a mad man. You almost knocked me over!'

'Sorry, Mr. White,' Aiden tried to catch his breath and compose himself.

'So what's the hurry?'

'I can't talk right now,' he tried to pass the businessman but he obstructed his path. Clyde White's eyes bore down upon him as if trying to extract information subliminally from his brain.

'Please, Mr. White, I have urgent news regarding the case. I must speak with the proper authorities.'

'Oh, give it up, Mr. Connelly. All this drama, it is just pathetic. You made a spectacle of yourself in the courtroom. You lost, deal with it.'

'OK, good advice,' he tried to pass again but Clyde White would not budge.

'So what is this urgent news regarding my son's death?'

'I've found the killer.'

'I know, glad you have finally accepted the truth. I'm looking forward to seeing her get what's coming to her.' An evil grin spread across his lined face.

'I mean the real killer'. disregarding etiquette and manners, Aiden slammed into Clyde White, sending the smartly dressed man hurtling to the ground as he ran past with just seconds to spare.

'Stop, stop everything!' He ran into the chamber where Brandy was being prepped. The morbid onlookers from the viewing room gasped in shock.

'You fool, someone get him out of here, he just attacked me!' Clyde White had caught up with him and was adding to the drama of the situation.

'Let her go,' he ordered the guards holding Brandy. She looked at him, her brown eyes full of confusion, then realization began to dawn in her.

'He told you?' her voice was soft.

'Yes, he did.' Aiden wanted to reach out and touch her, to take her in his arms and tell her that everything was going to be alright.

'Will somebody tell me what the hell is going on here?!' Clyde White yelled furiously.

'Allow me to explain,' Father West appeared in the doorway. He had gathered himself together and looked every inch the respectable priest.

'Father West, thank God, maybe you can help sort out this madness. They are shitting all over the memory of my son!'

'I'm sorry, Clyde.'

'It's alright, Father, just sort this mess out.'

175

'I'm sorry that I killed your son.'

Clyde White stared at Father West, too stunned to speak. The people in the viewing room looked on, speechless, their mouths agape. It was Aiden who broke the silence.

'Brandy is innocent, she never did anything.'

The guards, also in shock, released their grip on Prisoner 929 and she ran over to Aiden and collapsed in his arms.

'Thank you, thank you so much,' she cried.

'This is an outrage!' Clyde White was still struggling to take everything in. He turned to Father West.

'Why are you covering for her?'

'I'm not.'

'You are a man of God, you cannot kill somebody!'

'I'm sorry, Clyde, but I'm human. I can and I did kill somebody. I killed Brandon White and I'm willing to accept the consequences.' He turned to Brandy.

'You are such a beautiful, wonderful creature. You were willing to risk it all for me, but I couldn't let you do that. I hope you can forgive me.'

'For Christ's sake!' Clyde White punched Father West square in the jaw and the priest toppled over to the ground.

'He...he...' he looked at Brandy not quite knowing what to say. For so long he had seen her as the enemy, now to learn that she was also a victim was too overwhelming for him.

'Brandy White, you are finally free,' Aiden said to her. She clung to him with more ferocity and he felt like a hero.

'I'm so glad you came to Avalon,' she whispered.

'Yeah,' he mused. 'Me too.'

Chapter Thirteen

Unlucky for Some

Avalon had changed, and to Aiden, so had the entire world. Gone was his idyllic safe haven away from the city. In its place stood a town where even the most respected and unassuming members of society can be harboring the darkest of secrets. He realized with a heavy heart that deceit and corruption knows no bounds and can easily extend far beyond the reaches of the city and suburbia. He had been naïve to think that Avalon would be pure.

The perky female reporter found herself once more in the parking lot of Eastham Ladies Penitentiary with the cinder block castle as her backdrop.

'The small community of Avalon is still reeling after the shock confession to the murder of Brandon White by local priest, Patrick West.'

Since the revelation that he was the killer no one had referred to him as Father West. Nothing had been done officially, but in the hearts and minds of his parishioners he had already been stripped of his title and was now just an ordinary man; a man who they now loathed and resented. How quickly the masses can turn.

'Brandy White was originally found guilty of first degree murder, but now in a remarkable U-turn as a result of recent events, she is due today to walk away a free woman.'

Aiden smiled at the television screen. He was so happy for Brandy; she was finally free. She had the rest of her life to do whatever she wanted. Despite his glee that she was being released he felt strangely melancholic. He was draped across his

177

sofa starring at the television set in front of him. In the kitchen Isla was baking cookies with Meegan; they had not really spoken about all that happened. In all honesty, he was still trying to wrap his head around it all. More than anything he was confused by his feelings for Brandy. He loved her that much was true. But he was a married man with a young daughter, what happens now that she is a free woman? Free to live and love whomever she chooses? Would she want to be with him? Would he want to be with her? He knew that at some point he would have to address both Brandy and his feelings but he was procrastinating.

'Babe!' he called towards the kitchen.

'Could you bring me another beer?'

Trinity Church was in disarray. It had been predictably been targeted by vandals. The words Liar, Murderer and Devil were scrawled across the outside walls. Patrick West had let everyone down, most of all himself. He sat in his cell with nothing but time. Time to think, time to cry, time to sleep. Just time. He'd gone over things time and again in his mind; it was all going perfectly, no one had suspected him in the slightest. He just needed to keep his mouth shut until after Brandy was dead. Then he would repent to the Lord and all would be forgiven. But his guilty conscience had been burning away at his soul. Brandy White was many things but she was no killer. Day by day it was destroying him as he stood by his decision to let her take the fall. In the end he knew he had to act, no matter how dire the consequences would be. He could still see their faces all too clearly when he told them he was the killer. They had once held him in such high regard, looked at him with loving, kind eyes, but now he was the embodiment of the devil. He understood their anger, their hatred. But at the same time, the only thing he regretted was not speaking out sooner. He had lost his faith a long time ago; he only carried on because he felt that he had a duty to the community and that people needed him. Killing Brandon, it made him feel alive, more alive than he had ever felt in his entire life. He had never done anything remotely violent before and it scared him. Yet he was still glad that he did it. As soon as Brandy had told him of the abuse and that she lost her baby, he knew in his heart that Brandon deserved to die. It made him sick to see him sitting there in church week after week with his father, whilst poor Brandy was left at home, hiding her battered and bruised body away from the world. He wanted to expose Avalon's angel for who he truly was. But now Father West was the monster; somehow Brandon was still the victim in all of this. At least Brandy was free of their hatred; that gave him some comfort.

'I still can't believe that Father West could do such a thing,' Isla said as she handed her husband his second ice cold beer.

'Yeah, I know,' he muttered.

'You never gave up on her. Imagine if you had, she'd be dead now. That girl owes you her life.'

'She owes me nothing, it's my job.'

'Yeah, well you are very good at it! I'm proud of you!' She bent down and kissed him gently on his forehead. Guilt surged through him as he recalled his kiss with Brandy.

'Are you OK?' she asked, concerned.

'Yeah hun, just tired.'

'I bet you are, you deserve some rest.'

He had never felt so tired before in all his life, mentally that is, not physically. His brain ached with it all. He felt like wherever he turned people were excitedly discussing the Avalon scandal when all he wanted to do was get away from it. He had lived it, which was more than enough.

'Here she comes,' the reporter said excitedly, trying to push through the crowd to get to the halo of hair that had just left the prison gates.

'Brandy, Brandy!' she yelled.

Aiden switched off the television. He wasn't ready to see Brandy. At least not yet.

Brandy gazed around what was once her marital home. Over the past few months Brandon's parents had boxed up all their son's belongings so that all that remained was the shell of the house. She dropped down the duffel bag which contained her few worldly possessions and wandered over to the point where her husband breathed his last breath. The carpet had been cleaned, all traces of him gone. It was as if it had never happened. A sharp knock at the front door disturbed her from her thoughts.

'Oh, Aiden,' she beamed at her visitor.

Aiden Connelly's mind had been conflicted as to whether he should go and visit Brandy that day or not. In the end, he reasoned that he was her only friend and she would need him at this difficult time. He told Isla he was popping into work. He wasn't quite sure why he had lied to her; it was probably to avoid any confrontation. He drove out to what was once the home of the young Mr. and Mrs. White, a place that will forever be infamous for the tragedies that occurred within its walls.

'Brandy, hey, how are you?'

'Come in, come in,' she ushered him inside. He was surprised by how sparse the house was; there was only the bare minimum of furniture. He reasoned that Clyde White must have emptied the house out in anticipation of selling it on. No one ever believed that Brandy would be coming back to claim it.

'Pretty crowded in here, huh?' she joked.

'It's minimalist,' he laughed.

'I'd say sit down except there are no seats, and I'm afraid I'm fresh out of coffee, and pretty much everything else.'

'But you are free.'

'Am I?'

'Yeah, of course you are. You've been given an official pardon; your life is yours to live as you please for many years to come.'

'But here, in Avalon, I'll never be able to escape from it all. There will always be a black cloud following me around; people will always be looking at me, judging me.' She seemed so much older, wiser than she had in prison. Life was beginning to take its toll on her.

'So what now?'

'A fresh start,' she smiled at him and the brightness returned to her face.

'Where? Are you going to stay here?'

'I did a whole lot of thinking in prison. I've only ever known Avalon. I've never been on a boat, or a plane. I feel like life is giving me a second chance and I don't intend to waste it. I'm going to sell this place and move away.'

'Move away, where? When?' he didn't want her to leave. He had almost lost her once, he didn't want to lose her again.

'You inspired me, Aiden.'

'I did?'

'Yes, you did! You showed me that there are some people in the world who care, who are brave. I always thought that the city was full of shallow, cold people, but you are from the city and you are the kindest man I have ever met.'

'So where will you go?'

'I'm moving to Chicago.'

'But what will you do there?'

'It's funny; with all the television coverage someone out there recognized me and got in touch with the prison. Carol Cotton. She's my Ma's estranged sister, who knew? When she heard Brandy and Avalon she began piecing things together. She lives in Chicago and owns a successful beauty salon. Aiden, she's offered me a job! Isn't that great? A chance to start over!'

'Yeah, that is great,' he tried to sound happy for her.

'What's wrong?' she sensed his sadness.

'It's just…' he struggled to find the right words.

'Aiden, you know that I love you, with all my heart.' He smiled at this.

'But you have a wife and a little girl who need you. I've had enough trouble with men. I need to discover myself, find out who I am. I was always listening to other people, to my Ma, to Father West. This time I'm going to listen to me and do what I want.'

'I'm going to miss you so much,' he confessed.

'I'll miss you too, but I'll call, email, whatever it is city people do!' she laughed. Then the laughter faded and she regarded him with a more serious expression.

'You saved my life, Aiden Connelly. I owe you everything. I will never, ever forget you. You are truly the greatest man I have ever met.'

They embraced and he could feel her heart beating against his chest. She still had the same intoxicating scent of peaches and vanilla.

'You are heavenly, Brandy White,' he whispered.

'It's' Brandy Cotton now,' she informed him.

'Just so you know, you are a star that does sparkle. You shone out to me the day I met you and you really did light up my life.'

'Thank you,' she pulled away and smiled up at him. He felt the urge to kiss her but resisted.

'You have such a good heart, Aiden, don't let anything change that. You are the best thing that has ever happened to me.' He pulled her into his chest once more; he didn't want to let go.

'Do you think I'll like the city?'

'I think you'll love it.'

He wondered if city life would change Brandy, as it had once changed Isla. But if even prison could not stifle her spirit he knew in his heart that she would be fine.

'What's next for Aiden Connelly?'

'I honestly don't know.'

'Well, you can't leave Avalon. The people here need you.'

'They do?'

'Yeah! You stood up to Buck Fern and Clyde White. No one has ever dared to do that before. You have really shaken things up around here!'

They at last disconnected from one another and he reluctantly made his way to the door.

'Oh, do you know what else I'm going to do?'

'What?' he asked, intrigued.

'I've enrolled at a college in Chicago. I'm going to go back and get my high school diploma!' she was smiling at him and she was more luminous than ever. Looking at her, so beautiful and full of promise, he felt amazing. The world was no longer an evil place devoid of hope. She had restored his faith in humanity, in justice and in love.

'Are you an angel?' he asked and then laughed at how stupid he sounded.

'Nope, I'm just a twenty-four-year old widow with a whole lot of life that needs living!'

'Just don't go forgetting about me!'

'As if I could! Thank you for saving me, Aiden.'

'No problem, Brandy Cotton, it was my pleasure.'

As Aiden entered the kitchen of his home his senses were drenched in the sweet scent of freshly baked cakes. Pride of place in the middle of the table sat a delicious looking chocolate cake, with the words 'Love You Daddy,' scrawled on in icing.

'Do you like it?' Isla asked from the doorway, Meegan perched in her arms, watching her father's reaction excitedly.

'It's great! I can't believe that my girls did this for me!' Meegan leapt down from her mother and clumsily ran over to his waiting arms for a big cuddle.

'I made it just for you!' she told him happily.

'Does that mean that I get to eat it all?'

'Nooooo!'

'OK, OK, I'll share.' He smiled across to Isla, she looked tired and weary.

'Sweetheart, why don't you go upstairs and play with your toys for a little bit.' She obeyed him and toddled off towards her room.

'So…it's all over now then?' Isla asked nervously. In her heart she knew that she was questioning if more than the trial was over. She was a woman; she felt things. She had tried to ignore the way Aiden looked when he spoke about Brandy, how he had been on the verge of a breakdown at the thought of losing her. She didn't want to admit it, but she could feel him slipping away from her.

'Yeah, the trial is all over. Brandy is a free woman now; it's great.'

'Have you been to see her?' there was an accusing tone in her voice.

'Yeah, just before, to straighten out some legal crap. You know how it is.'

'You work so hard,' she said bitterly.

They were silent for a moment, each contemplating their next move in their own mind. The soft humming of a contented little girl playing with her dolls danced down the stairs and lay between them.

'She's very beautiful,' Isla commented.

'Who?'

'Brandy.'

'Isla…' he put up his hands in frustration, he could tell where this was going and he didn't have the energy for it.

'Do you love her?' the question was so direct that it caught him off guard. He looked at Isla, his wife, the mother of his child. He saw in her face part of his own history, and in Meegan he saw his future. Brandy was right about him; he was a good man, which meant that there was only one answer which he could give.

'No! Don't be ridiculous, I love you,' the lie burnt his throat as he released it.

'Oh, Aid,' she ran over, relieved, and melted into her husband's arms.

'I'm sorry to question you, I really am. I'm so silly. Forgive me?'

'Of course,' and he kissed her. He felt like a fraud.

'We can get back to how we were, when things were good,' she pressed herself harder against him. Part of him wanted that, to have things return to how they once were. Perhaps, in time, his feelings for Brandy would dull and he could happily play the role of dutiful husband and doting father.

'Have you seen Father West?'

'No,' he answered, grateful for the change in the topic of conversation. 'If I never see that man again that is fine by me.'

'But he came good in the end,' Isla challenged.

'Imagine, if he had never come forward, what would have happened?' For a moment, her darker side lured its wicked head once more and she thought of what could have been. A world without Brandy, was that really such a bad place? Father West had seemed like such a good man, and the people in the town loved him so. Now Avalon was in turmoil, not one but two of their heroes had been disgraced and the local tramp now once more crowned a queen.

'What will Brandy do now?'

'She's going to live in Chicago, sample city life.'

'And what about us? Are we going to stay in Avalon?'

Aiden pondered the question for a moment. His expectations of country life had certainly not been met. Whilst he enjoyed the

184

fresh, clean air and the abundance of nature he was sure that he would still be regarded as a villain and an outsider by many of the residents for years to come. He had made enemies of Buck Fern and Clyde White, who remained heavyweights of the Avalon community; his wife had even feared for her safety at one point. What was keeping them there?

'I don't know, we could always move.'

'Again? I don't think so, Aid.'

'Do you like it here?' He sadly realized that he had never before asked his wife how she was feeling about living in Avalon.

'I'm getting to like it,' she smiled. 'I've enrolled Meegan at a lovely pre-school which she starts next week and Edmond and his wife have invited us over for a barbeque this weekend. I think that we are finally starting to settle in.'

'Decision's made then, we stay.'

Aiden lay awake that night, as he did many nights. The crickets hummed outside his window, oblivious to all that had occurred in their small town. A gentle breeze fanned the curtains and tickled his skin. Earlier, in the gentle light of dusk he had driven around town to clear his head; he noticed a group of people furiously scrubbing the graffiti off Trinity Church. The world was beginning to return to normal and Aiden and his family were now a part of it. Isla was lost in a deep sleep as he waded through his forest of thoughts. Tired of the sound of his own concerns echoing in his head he got up and wandered softly into his daughter's room to watch Meegan sleeping. She was so peaceful, so innocent; his very own Avalon angel who needed him more than anybody else in the whole world. Brandy could find her own way now, his daughter needed him; he knew where he was supposed to be.

'Good to see you, Mr. Connelly,' Betty smiled warmly at him as he entered Cope and May Attorneys at Law.

'You too, Betty,' he replied, thankful that she was no longer angry towards him. All day around town people had been smiling at him, wishing him good day. It was a much needed change from the bitter stares and cold silences. He was beginning to once more feel a part of Avalon.

'Aiden, my dear boy,' Edmond wrapped his arms around his young colleague before he was even fully through the door to the office.

'You did a splendid job, splendid, getting Father West to confess to it all like you did!'

'Well, he came forward himself.'

'Don't be so modest! You are a modern day Atticus Finch!'

'I wouldn't say that,' Aiden blushed.

'This is a time to rejoice! You have put Cope and May back on the map! Betty has been inundated, poor girl, with calls from people eager to have us represent them. Glorious, simply glorious!'

'I'm just glad to help.'

'And helped you have, my lad! Come, come, a toast,' Edmond handed Aiden a mug where a dash of hard liquor sat nestled at the bottom, golden and pure. For a brief moment, Aiden thought sadly of his favorite blue mug, which was no more. Change was inevitable. the skill to getting through life unscathed was learning to adapt to it.

'To my colleague and friend, Aiden Connelly,' the two men chinked mugs before knocking back their contents. He coughed as the amber nectar burnt his throat.

'It's strong stuff,' Edmond chuckled.

'Sure is,' Aiden wheezed, struggling to find his voice.

'I take it you are planning on staying here in Avalon? I know it hasn't been an easy introduction to the town and you had to take a whole load of crap off people, so I'd understand if you were thinking of heading back to the city.'

'No, I've been doing some thinking and here is where I want to be for now.'

'Well, that's great news. Since you are staying, you'll be needing this,' Edmond passed Aiden a brown file.

'What's this?'

'Your next case.'

Aiden flicked open the file and scanned the first page with interest.

'Custody case?' he raised his eyebrows to Edmond.

'Yeah, quite high profile. A wealthy couple who live just out of town, he's old and loaded, she's young and stunning. She's

186

been wed to him for a few years, given him two kids and now wants out. However, the old man wants full custody, says she isn't a fit mother, that sort of thing.'

'So, I'm representing the mother?'

'No, that'd be too easy, our client is the father. I figured that you are ready to handle the tough cases now.'

'I've never seen a father be awarded full custody before.'

'Well, just see what you can do. This isn't an open, shut case but it should be a whole lot less aggravation than the White murder case.'

'I'll do my best. What's the guy's name?'

'You are going to love this,' Edmond smiled conspiratorially.

'His name is Samuel Fern.'

'Fern?' Aiden echoed, shocked.

'As in...?'

'As in the one and only. He is Buck Fern's older brother. I told you that this was a small town.'

Aiden Connelly was finally free from the rat race, yet his troubles had followed him from the city and into the country. He sat with the sun on his face, a beer in his hand, contemplating life in general. In the distance, his wife pushed their young daughter on a swing. The child's jubilant giggles floated over to him on a gentle summer breeze. It was perfect. Yet his heart ached; he thought of Brandy, off in the city, and wondered what she was doing, who she was meeting. He tilted his head to gaze up into the cloudless sky, a vast amazing blue which seemed to go on forever. He had decided to take Samuel Fern's case even though he knew it wouldn't be easy. The warmth from the sun delighted his senses. Despite the clear skies he sensed change in the air, or perhaps it was just within himself. His adventures in Avalon were just beginning.